Poppy Curses and Emerald Skies

CHELSEA BIDDISCOMBE

This is a work of fiction. Similarities to real people, places, or events are entirely coincidental.

POPPY CURSES AND EMERALD SKIES

First Edition, June 24th, 2024

ISBN 978-1-7383001-2-9

Copyright © 2024 by Chelsea Biddiscombe

Cover by Marina

All rights reserved.

No portion of this book may be reproduced in any form without written permission from the publisher or author, except as permitted by U.S. copyright law.

Contents

Dedication	VII
Prologue	1
1. Chapter 1	9
2. Chapter 2	19
3. Chapter 3	27
4. Chapter 4	35
5. Chapter 5	45
6. Chapter 6	57
7. Chapter 7	65
8. Chapter 8	71
9. Chapter 9	81
10. Chapter 10	91

11. Chapter 11	97
12. Chapter 12	105
13. Chapter 13	111
14. Chapter 14	119
15. Chapter 15	129
16. Chapter 16	137
17. Chapter 17	147
18. Chapter 18	153
19. Chapter 19	161
20. Chapter 20	167
21. Chapter 21	171
22. Chapter 22	175
23. Chapter 23	181
24. Chapter 24	189
25. Chapter 25	197
26. Chapter 26	209
27. Chapter 27	213
Epilogue	219
Gratitude	225
About the Author	227

Where can you find Chelsea?	229
Translations	231
Other Works by Chelsea Biddiscombe	233

Dedication

This my love letter to Oz, to the aurora borealis, and to the dreamers of the world.

To Chelsea from thirty years ago – We made it to Oz, kid. I couldn't have done it without you. Thank you for always holding on to the dream.

Prologue

Lightening streaked across the sky and thunder shook the ground. The wind whipped leaves, dust, and dirt into mini cyclones as rain drops pelted every available surface and exploded upon impact. It was the kind of rain that would leave welts on skin if someone was unlucky enough to be caught out in it.

Every creature with a lick of sense had already found shelter, a safe spot to wait out the storm, knowing that this wasn't a storm made up of completely natural sources. It had come on far too quickly and seemed to build with rage. The wind whistled and screamed through every door crack and window crevice. Families huddled together under blankets, watching the flames flicker on the candles lit for comfort.

Parents comforted their kids while sparing glances at each other, sending silent signals to each other that something wasn't right. Even the smallest of creatures, the feral cats and the feeble mice, were huddling together for comfort.

Up at the castle a different kind of storm roared, wreaking havoc and bringing its own kind of devastation. The speed of the wind and falling rain was so fast that doors started flying open by mere force, slamming against stone walls. Every crack of thunder made it sound as if boulders were being crashed together, and branches of trees were flying past windows on the third and fourth floors. If the storm didn't pass soon the roof threatened to lift right off, exposing every inhabitant to the harshness outside.

In a cold stone room three behemoth fae men were quickly scurrying around, gathering ingredients from glass jars that sat on dusty shelves against the exterior walls. With every thunder boom the jars wobbled, causing them to constantly be clinking together, not that the occupants of the room paid any attention to the noise. Speed was of the upmost importance if they were to be successful, as time was running out to call for aid.

"Hurry! Bring the crystal over here!" Gunner barked to the others as he pulled a small cauldron out from underneath a sturdy worktable. Beside him he placed an old, worn book and, as his shaking clumsy fingers started flipping through pages, looking for a spell he knew to be there, Gunner kept glancing towards the door to make sure no one had followed them.

"We don't have everything we need!" Callan's voice shook as he limped around the room, looking through all the glass jars a second time for what they needed. Some of the jars sat empty; not the fault of anyone, just the result of poor timing. There hadn't been a supply restock in weeks and now they knew it was because their supply runs were being ransacked and destroyed.

"Doesn't matter, we'll have to make do. We're out of time!" Rune stated as he grabbed ingredients off the shelves by the handful. He had spent much of his time in this room; it was second nature for him, and he barely had to look at the jars to know what ingredients he was pulling out. Both Rune and

Callan shuffled over to Gunner, tossing ingredients in undetermined amounts into the cauldron.

"How did this happen? How did they get past our defenses?" Callan's voice started shaking with adrenaline and fear. Looking over at Gunner, Callan was assessing the injuries displayed on his face. They were all taken by surprise and, while they were all warriors in their own rights, the forces that fought them for control seemed powered by something darker, and it tore right through them.

"I don't know. Better question, how did they get past *his* defenses? He's supposed to be the strongest one out of all of us." The disbelief dripped out of Gunner's voice. Taking a pestle Gunner started smashing the ingredients together to make a paste. Time wasn't a luxury that they had now that the enemy had broken through every barrier and torn through every defence put in place to protect them.

"Did you see him in there? They completely incapacitated him!" Rune couldn't control the anger in his voice, but he kept his feet moving. He expected more of their King, but if he was being honest the disappointment he felt was directed inwards just as much as it was outwards. They had all trained together their entire lives; every day for years they went through battle training and strategy sessions, where they pulled apart every battle written in the history books.

As a group, they would take a battle and create a defense plan that would have had the losing side turn the tides. After all that they were blind to the betrayal within and being completely blindsided had weakened them. Shaking his head to clear his thoughts, Rune again scolded himself. They didn't have time to let worry cloud their thoughts or they would never finish their task in time.

"We shouldn't have run without him!" Banging his fists on the table, shaking the cauldron, Callan couldn't let it go. It was drilled into him from birth, never abandon the King. Fight to your death to defend him, if need be. When the time came, the three of them took the opportunity to run. Disgraceful was what it was. The only hope he was holding on to was that the enemy would need their King alive for whatever they were planning.

"What did you expect us to do? We have one shot at this, and if we fail our whole kingdom will be turned from paradise into a nightmare, more so than it already is, and the people will suffer more than they've ever imagined they could. We have one shot at this, with or without him, so will you stop wasting time and focus!" Gunner set Callan straight, much like when they were growing up. Callan had always looked up to Gunner, treated him like an older brother. Gunner was never afraid to pick a fight and everything Callan had learned about standing his ground came from watching the example Gunner set.

The howling wind outside picked up in strength, but in the distance they could hear the rhythmic stomping of soldiers coming their way. It was accompanied by the taunting laugh of the last person they wanted to see.

Suddenly the window coverings all flew open at the same time, blowing out all of the candles lighting the room. Callan and Rune ran around, closing the covers and latching them shut once again. The air in the dark room became thick and the only light sneaking in through the cracks in the window covers was coming from the lightning in the sky, leaving them with only their fae sight to find their way around.

Once Gunner had pulverized the ingredients, he found a box of matches hidden underneath the table. Pulling it out he lit a match and dropped it into the cauldron. The concoction immediately burst into green and black flame.

"Rune, toss the crystal into the mixture. We need to put the flames out once it's in there, and then all that's left is the incantation." Rune did as Gunner asked and tossed a cherry sized crystal into the cauldron. It sank into the fiery potion and only when it was completely covered did Gunner use the little magic he had left to put the fire out. Just as he was about to pull the crystal out, the door to the room blew open with enough force that the three of them were sent flying in three different directions across the room.

The outline of the one person they feared most filled the doorway, backlit from the torches in the hall. Taking a moment to look around the room, she let out a malicious laugh. Where her sister was, they didn't know but she wouldn't be far behind.

"Looks like I found you in time. Pity, I thought you gentlemen were going to put up a better fight than this." Her sickly-sweet voice sent chills down their spines. Stepping into the room she carried her broom made of branches, twigs, and straw in her left hand, leaving her right hand free for any combat.

Callan was the first to recover, getting up and lunging for her with his fists up, but with the flick of her wrist he was thrown headfirst into a stone wall, effectively knocking him unconscious.

Rune let out a battle cry as he got up and, in a fit of rage, he grabbed the cauldron and tried swinging it at her head. Already predicting his moves, the Enchantress started singing an incantation in an ancient language.

"Abdita tempore, latens in spatio. Auxilium vocamus...." An invisible force stopped Rune where he stood and refused to allow him to move a muscle. The pot fell from his hands as his body shook with effort. Rune was trying to fight the magic, but it was obvious by how hard his limbs were shaking and how red his face was getting, from straining, that Rune was failing.

Gunner looked up from where he was thrown on the floor, and noticed the Enchantress was distracted with Rune's attempt at fighting back. Gunner subtly looked across the floor to where the forgotten crystal had rolled after falling out of the cauldron that Rune dropped. Covered in debris and the potion it was tossed in, the crystal sat there with more supernatural power than the natural world ever bestowed upon it. Even with the wind whipping around and the evil bitch laughing at their misfortune, Gunner could hear the whispers coming from the crystal.

"*Save us…help us…send us aid…*" Crawling across the floor slowly to not draw much attention to himself, he got close enough to put his hand on it. It felt warm to the touch. Gunner started whispering an incantation.

"Corde puro, exaudi vocationem nostram." Gunner whispered it over and over, clutching the crystal tightly in his hand.

Rune saw out of the corner of his eye what Gunner was up to and did his best to keep all the Enchantresses attention on himself. Reaching deep down into himself, to the very bottom of his magic, Rune could feel the last spark of it trying to survive. He grabbed a hold of it, pulling it up with him as hard as he could. Up and up, he pulled on that spark, until finally he could feel it start to warm the palms of his hands. He only had enough power for one shot, so he had to take his time and make it count. Everything was depending on it.

"Is that all you've got, you wicked bitch?" Rune called out to the Enchantress, waiting for the perfect moment to strike. One thing the Enchantress couldn't stand being was being disrespected, and Rune had always provided her with a challenge. When she took a step towards him Rune knew this was his last chance. He clenched his fists, using the vibrations in his magic to break the hold the Enchantress had placed on him. Holding his left hand up, praying the hit landed, he summoned every last scrap of energy and power into an energy ball the size of an apple and flung it in the general direction of the Enchantress, who redirected it away from herself without much effort.

When the last of his power hit the ground and disappeared, it took the last of his hope with it. His shoulder sagged and his heart hurt at the knowledge that he would not be walking away from this battle.

The Enchantress laughed at his pathetic attempt of a fight, curling her lips into a cruel smile.

"Failed again, Rune? Tsk tsk tsk. It's starting to become a habit." With that she sent a pulse of energy at Rune, the result throwing him into the broken armoire behind him. A piece of the cabinet had broken off and was now sticking out from his body. Rune looked down in disbelief at the piece of furniture protruding from his chest. His breath started getting shallower and the last thing Rune saw before loosing consciousness was his own blood starting to seep out around the edges of the wound.

Two down, one to go. The Enchantress turned her attention to Gunner, and upon seeing what he was holding, and the chanting she could now hear him performing under his breath, she instantly tried to separate him from the crystal by throwing him across the room with the flick of her wrist.

However, she was a moment too late. A small glow had formed in the centre of the crystal, and as Gunner held his hand out the crystal dissolved into thin air.

A meteor lit up the sky as it streaked across the storm clouds, witnessed by the people of a nation holding on to nothing but hope and each other. They saw the light, knew what it meant, and crossed their fingers that help wouldn't come to late.

Gunner only had a mere moment to feel victorious before the Enchantress had a foot on his chest, using her magic to keep him pinned.

"How brave of you, to openly defy me like this. Let's do something about that, shall we?" A moment later Gunner's screams could be heard throughout the night air, louder than the storm, and the citizens of Oz could only imagine what horrors were happening in that castle.

When she was done with him, Gunner was left bruised and broken on the floor. His bones were shattered, and his breath was coming in shallow pants. All he could manage was looking out the window at the sky. He stared at the path that the meteor made through the storm clouds, knowing that his suffering could possibly end, if only the army who found that crystal would answer the call.

Chapter 1

Dori sat straight up in her bed, sweat rolling down her forehead and getting caught in her curly auburn hair. Her freckled face was damp, and her breath was coming in fast.

Glancing outside, through the window on the wall in front of her, at the dark void that was the forest on the west edge of her property, it felt like something dark was looking back. The trees were swaying in the wind, causing the shadows to sway back and forth. Always the one with the overactive imagination, Dori had to force herself to look away before she started believing that she could see creatures lurking behind those trees.

Sighing to herself and looking at her clock, which read 3 a.m., Dori was more awake and alert than she wanted to be. Giving in to the idea that there was no getting back to sleep any time soon with the way her heart was pumping, Dori sat up straighter and started taking a few deep breaths.

Her pulse was still racing, and her hands were shaking as Dori reached up and rubbed the sleep from her eyes, desperately trying to remember what it was that she was dreaming about. Everything was fading from her memory faster than she could recall it. Dori swung her legs down from the bed and braced herself as she put her bare feet on the cold, wooden floor. Standing up and shuffling out of her small bedroom to the kitchen sink, Dori retrieved a glass from the cabinet, along the way, and filled it with cool water from the tap. She paused for a moment and took a few sips to calm down her breathing.

As she heard the wind start to pick up, causing the window shutters to shake, Dori took a good look around at her home. Her house was built more than a few decades ago, giving it a unique kind of charm. The downside was that all the rooms were built small, even the bathroom barely had the space for a decent sized tub. Living on her own, however, meant that she didn't mind the lack of space.

The kitchen window had the best view of the open night sky, pointing toward the farmers field to the north of where she lived. Dori had added some white, frilly lace curtains to that window, with small sunflowers imprinted on them. Living out in the country meant that she didn't think much of putting blinds on every window for privacy.

There was rarely anyone else around. That left Dori able to keep most of her curtains open during the day, for the sunlight, and at night it always left her with the most fantastical views of the night sky. Without the city lights to drown it out, Dori was able to view the stars and planets in all their glory most nights.

There was something to be said about staring at the stars, in the middle of the country, without another human within a fifty-mile radius. It filled Dori with wonder and made her feel like maybe there was a bit of magic alive in the world. The way that the constellations seemed to twinkle and take on a life of their own was enchanting.

Dazed and still focusing on her breathing and her wandering mind, Dori almost missed the bright light that flit across the sky. It was a vibrant green and was moving fast. She immediately became alert as she watched an object fall from the moving light in the sky and directly into her yard. It didn't make a sound as it buried itself in the overgrown weeds and damp earth out in her front yard. Dori stared at where it fell for a full minute, not sure if she had seen something or if her tired eyes were playing tricks on her.

Whatever had fallen was sitting slightly on her side of the property, just before the farmers field began. Dori had to blink a few times before it occurred to her that, whatever it was, it was still emanating a green glow, which looked as bright as a beacon in the dark of the night.

Dori's curious nature only let her slightly hesitate before she made her way towards her front door, slipping on her spring flannel jacket and tucking her feet into her ankle-high muck boots. As she opened the door one last thought crossed her mind: that whatever had fallen from the sky should maybe be left alone. Maybe it wasn't something for her to mess with. That thought lasted for a mere second before Dori pushed herself out the door and into the dead of night, with no one around to stop her. Curiosity won out, as it often did when it came to Dori.

She tip-toed across her own yard, as if the suction sound of her boots stomping through the mud would alert some invisible force that would question her on why she was out at this time of night. The night air held a chill and had her shaking slightly inside her jacket. Step after step Dori tried coming up with a logical reason for something that fell from the sky to be glowing as brightly as the mystery object was.

As she stepped closer to the edge of her property, Dori started hearing a slight buzzing coming from the ground. Knowing it was not late enough in the spring for insects to be very active, Dori was at a loss for an answer. Once she was close enough to be standing over top of the object, Dori stopped and stared down for a moment.

Taking her eyes off of it and looking left and right to see if anyone else was around--which was ridiculous because it was the middle of the night and Dori's closest neighbours lived a few minutes down the road--Dori realized the sound had stopped. How odd. She turned her head back to the object only to hear the strange sound start up again. Everything about this object seemed to be designed to draw her in, and it was working.

Bending down, but careful not to put her knees into the wet grass, Dori tried to get a closer look at the object. Thankful that it still had a slight glow, Dori could see it under the weeds and dirt that it had gotten tangled with. Reaching out to brush the dirt off of it she stopped herself. Dori was curious, but she prided herself on not being completely stupid. While highly unlikely, whatever this object was could have been radioactive, or have some type of space disease on it, and she did not want to be scooping that up in her hands.

Looking around Dori spotted a stick from the wood pile not far from her. She quickly got up, scurried to the wood pile, and picked it up. Hurrying back to her original spot, Dori squatted back down and started poking through the grass where the green light was coming from.

The stick scratched against something hard under the weeds, almost rock-like in its weight, as Dori tried pushing it around to get a better look at it. It was small and it was solid. Between the light coming from it and the dirt it had gathered falling into the field, it was hard for Dori to get a look at what it was.

Reaching in her jacket pocket for anything to help her pick it up Dori found a stray black glove left over from winter. Using the stick she carefully managed to push the item into the glove, using the glove itself as a carrying case.

Standing up her knees cracked, a sign that the cold and her age were both working against her. Turning back towards the house Dori started muttering to herself as her heart felt like it was beating out of her chest.

"Way to go, D, strange rock from space and you pick it up. It probably has some kind of space germs on it that are leeching through the glove and onto your skin right now." Still, even with her doubts, there was a feeling in the pit of her stomach that told her this item wouldn't hurt her. That this item was meant to be in her possession.

Once back inside she took it right to the sink, not even bothering to take off her boots or jacket. Turning on the warm water Dori timidly pushed the object out of her glove and onto the bottom of her kitchen sink, where it fell with a small thud. As the mud and muck started to wash off the object, Dori started inspecting the glove for any sign of danger.

The glove itself didn't look any different. There were no holes from something trying to burn through, the glove didn't have a strange or chemical smell to it either. While logic would tell her to still not touch it, as there were many odourless dangers that could have covered the object, there was something in her heart telling her otherwise. Some voice, a feeling, inside her heart telling her that this object was of no danger to her.

As strange as it sounded, the longer she looked at the object the more at peace she felt around it, as if being in its presence was enough to dull any concern that Dori may have had about it being dangerous. In fact, it was starting to look harmless to her, causing Dori to feel slightly ashamed of the drastic measures she took to bring it inside.

And with a history of making more mistakes than she cared to admit, she reached out into the water at the bottom of her sink and picked the object up with her bare hands. It was almost weightless and still covered in a fair bit of grime. It was surprisingly cool to the touch, but the moment it came into contact with her skin the slight glow that led Dori to it went out. Dori almost dropped it in surprise, but now that she was holding it, she didn't want to let go.

In an effort to fully see the object for what it was, Dori placed the object back under the stream of water, using her thumbs to wipe away more of the dirt. The more she wiped the more she saw the most spectacular colour coming through. Whatever the object was, it held rich green hues beneath the dirt. Taking her time and checking to make sure that the gentle water wasn't, in fact, damaging the object, Dori turned it around in her hands multiple times, gently cleaning as she went.

In the end the object was a small, cherry-sized, green and black lump of...what? She didn't know. It was strange but despite having only found this object less than an hour ago Dori felt such a resonance coming from it. A hum or vibration that she felt more than heard. If she stared at it, focused on it and nothing else, it was almost as if this small green rock was trying to talk to her.

Trying to keep her mind as calm as she could while dozens of scenarios danced in her head, Dori placed the green rock at the back of her counter, a place where it wasn't in any danger of rolling or falling off.

Crossing the room, still in her jacket and boots, Dori sat on her couch and stared at it from afar. It wasn't every day that a green rock fell from the sky, especially one this gorgeous. Was there something in space that exploded that didn't make the news? Did a bird pick it up from some place and hold on to it just long enough to bring it her way? Maybe it was a star that had fallen from the heavens only to land in her backyard. Was it the only one of its kind, or were other pieces of it falling out of the sky, baffling others?

Grabbing her phone from the small, brown coffee table, Dori set out to do what every person her age knew to do in situations they couldn't understand. She turned to the internet to see if someone else had answers. First, she tried searching for any strange happenings in her town. When that didn't work, she started to search for explosions in space scattering green tinted rocks or crystals. Once again, nothing showed up.

Sighing, Dori put her phone down and looked back up at the crystal. At least, that's what she decided it was. Maybe not an authentic emerald, but it sure had all the features of one. Looking across the room Dori's eyes landed on the crystal as a ringing started in her ears.

It started low, almost like the buzzing of a fly somewhere in the room, but the longer she stared at the crystal the louder it got. It became loud enough that Dori tried to drown out the noise by putting her hands over her ears, but that almost made it worse. The buzzing started to morph, and Dori could make out individual voices, all calling for help.

"Save us! Someone please help us! Help! Anyone, please!!!" Voices, one after another, started talking over one another, desperately pleading. Dori could barely make out individual words after a moment, so many voices blending together, sounding terrified and hurt. So many voices, asking for help. Men, women, and children, all begging for help. Not only could Dori hear them, but she could also feel what they were feeling. Her heart was breaking at the terror that started running through their veins. The anxiety, the depression, and the fear that each one of them was feeling.

Before she could comprehend what was happening her hands started to burn. Her fingertips that she so gently used to clean the crystal of its dirt started to almost buzz. Yet, with all of this going on, Dori had a hard time taking her eyes off the crystal.

It was only when her body, in an attempt to protect itself from whatever was causing harm, fell to the floor and curled into a ball, that she lost sight of the object. Immediately everything stopped. The ringing, the voices, the burning, all of it turned off as if someone had just twisted the knob on a tap.

Out of breath Dori sat on her floor for a moment, unable to move. Slowly she pulled her hands away from her ears and looked them over. There was nothing there, nothing noticeably different. She was prepared to see severe burns--at least that was what the pain had prepared her for--but there was nothing but a dull ache to remind her that something insane had just happened. Or had it?

Was it a hallucination of some type? Nothing about this night was making sense, so maybe this was all a dream. Slowly she started to stand, her legs shaking as if to tell her they couldn't hold her up for long. Dori's ears had a slight ache to them, as if she had stood out in a strong wind all day.

Dori refused to look over at the crystal, but it was making itself known. Something about it kept drawing her eyesight back, and after having to divert her stare for a fifth time, Dori had had enough.

She stood up and stomped over to the counter, swiping a towel off the side of the stove as she walked by it, and using the towel to cover the crystal. The peace and the silence that had greeted her brought back a sense of calm to Dori. Taking a moment while standing at the sink, she started looking back outside at the night sky. There was no sign of anything else falling from the sky. There was no sign that anything odd had taken place in her home.

Dori turned her eyes back to the towel, trying to almost stare a hole in it to see if looking at the crystal really caused that type of a reaction. There was a sense of fear that shot up her spine when she thought to herself, just one more look. After one more look, she could draw a conclusion about the object, decide what to do with it, and go to bed.

The moment that thought dawned on her it was as if someone else had control of her arm; her hand reached out and snatched the towel from the crystal. Dori's natural reaction was to shut her eyes and turn her head away. When nothing appeared to be happening Dori opened one of her hazel eyes and searched around. Everything looked normal and she looked crazy. Opening her other eye, it seemed as if her small kitchen was still the safe place she thought it was. Then she fully looked down at the crystal.

The strength at which the shouting and ringing in her ears returned and the burning on her hands flared up in pain almost threw her right to the floor. Her body's fight or flight instinct urged her to destroy the crystal, and her brain agreed that smashing it on the floor would be the quickest way to accomplish that. Dori's hand shot out, grabbed the crystal, and as if her hand on the crystal completed a circuit, her entire body jolted and before she blacked out, she heard one last voice.

"My kingdom doesn't deserve this."

Chapter 2

The whisper of a sweeter wind was enough to rouse Dori from what seemed like a deep and restful sleep. A sleep she would have appreciated more had she known how little she would be getting in the coming days.

The bed she was on seemed slightly damp, but not in an unpleasant way. In the distance, she could hear a strange bird's song, one that was softer and more delicate than anything she had heard before. Confusion started to set in when she moved her hand and felt strands of something tickle her fingers. Peeking her eyes open, not quite remembering what had happened the night before, Dori jolted awake the moment her eyes gazed at a tent of tall, swaying trees instead of her bedroom ceiling. Dori sat up with an urgency, trying desperately to make sense of what her eyes were seeing.

All around her were trees of various shapes and sizes. There were pines trees, birch trees, and spruce trees all circling the small clearing she was in. The soft bed she thought she was on turned out to be a bed of long, sweet smelling wild grass and clover.

Wildflowers grew all around in the most perfect variety of pastels. Pinks and purples, yellows and soft oranges, all mixed together. As the air moved around her Dori could smell the soft perfume the flowers were giving off, and it produced the feeling of comfort and hope inside of her. Butterflies and dragonflies, more than she had ever seen in her life, fluttered around the flowers in their own dance. Across the clearing, just for a moment, she saw what she thought was a deer peeking out from behind the brush. A moment later it was gone.

The bird's call in the distance started getting closer and was joined with another and another until it seemed like a choir was singing in the forest. The sunbeams dipped in and out of the leaves of the tall trees as they lightly danced in the wind.

Dori slowly stood up trying to make sense of it all. A slight dizziness stalled her for a minute, and she had to close her eyes until it passed. Once more she opened her eyes and, as she looked around, Dori realized that something was clenched in the palm of her left hand. Almost afraid to see what it was, Dori stared at her own fist. Her fingers were starting to ache with the pressure that she was using to hold them closed.

Slowly, Dori started to unfurl them, and the sun took that moment to reflect off of the green crystal in her hand. She looked down upon it and her memory of the previous evening came back to her. The strange light falling from the sky, the awful ringing in her ears, the scared voices screaming for help, and the burning of her palms. How had she gotten from there to here, in the middle of some type of meadow?

The sunrays were starting to warm up her skin and Dori realized she was still in the outfit from the night before. Wearing her spring jacket and muck boots, her sleep clothes were peeking out from underneath. Did she walk here from her house? Nothing around her looked very familiar or sounded familiar.

She would have had to have walked quite awhile, and how did no one stop her to see if she was alright?

Dori looked around the clearing that she seemed to be in. She was definitely in the forest somewhere. Hopefully she wouldn't be running into any bears or wildlife that would be less than excited to see her. Checking all her pockets to see what she had with her, Dori realized that her only possessions were the clothes on her back and the crystal in her hand. Nothing to defend herself with and nothing for her to call for help with.

Taking a moment to assess herself, searching her body for any injuries, Dori concluded she wasn't at all injured. Even her hands seemed to be in good working order. Inside, however, she was a mess. The urge to absolutely panic at being lost and experiencing memory gaps was strong.

The crystal kept staring back at her from her left hand, taunting her, urging her forward, but with no idea of where she was it would only be a guess on which way forward was. Dori wanted to toss the stupid crystal into the bush, to get it out of her life. A small part of her kept asking 'what if'. What if this crystal had some importance that she couldn't see yet? What if this crystal was the answer to some unknown riddle? The debate went round and round in her head until she was almost dizzy from it.

In the end Dori decided to hold on to it. Not in case she needed it later, but because without the crystal there, physically in her possession, Dori might start to believe that everything that had happened the night before was one bad dream.

A sharp hammering started in the distance, breaking Dori out of her inner dialogue. A spike of hope brewed up inside as Dori decided that a noise like that meant people were nearby, and people meant help, or at least answers on where she was, so she started walking towards the noise. If she could find someone else out here, perhaps she could have them give her a lift home.

Dori started walking through the bush in the direction that she believed the sound to be coming from. The trees and bush seemed to be getting thicker as she went. The moss on the forest floor almost seemed to be pulling her down, making it harder and harder for her to pull her feet up and out. But she was determined to find that sound before it disappeared. One foot after the other Dori moved through the forest.

The warm sun that had helped wake her up was now covered up by some of the fluffiest white and grey clouds. The closer to the sound that she got, the wilder the forest around her seemed to get. The birds that had sounded so melodic previously now sounded harsh and shrill. The soft, sweet grass was slowly being replaced by prickly weeds and almost cactus-like plants.

Through Dori's ragged breathing and the less than graceful way she was stomping through the forest, a new sound emerged. A slow, deep growl started to come from behind her. Dori had almost missed it, being focused more on her own noises. However, all it took was a brief second for the sound to reach her ears. Dori paused all motion and heavy breathing for a moment before her body decided it didn't want to be around when whatever was making that sound found it's way to her.

Dori turned and started running towards the hammering, as fast as she could go. Her legs were starting to tire, her lungs felt as if they were going to explode, but she kept pressing on, the will to live stronger than the will to discover what was making the rumbling noise. Curiosity be damned, hers certainly seemed to have damned her the night before.

Dori's mind was spinning with all different ideas on what was behind her. It could be bears, it could be something else entirely. Cougars, mountain lions, or something worse. Until she knew where she was it was hard to decide what dangers lurked inside the forest that she seemed stuck in.

Not paying much attention to where she was going, it came as a surprise to Dori when the forest floor was very quickly cut off and, instead, Dori found herself standing on the side of a road. The road in question was a bit of an unusual one; it wasn't a dirt road or one made of concrete. Instead, it seemed to be fashioned out of dirty, yellow bricks.

A tiny idea tickled the back of her mind, telling her that she had heard a story long ago of such a road, but Dori didn't have time to entertain stories from her childhood, and instead she made the split-second decision to follow this road towards the hammering noise to see if it would lead her to some type of civilization.

After one more vicious growl from behind her, whatever beast had tried to pursue her had backed off. The clouds were still covering the sun, but the air seemed almost lighter. The hammering sound made its way back to Dori and she found it was quite close. This gave her hope that she would be able to find someone soon, which was good because she was very ready to go home. Her feet ached and her stomach growled, reminding her that she didn't know when the last time she had eaten was. Her mouth felt dry and pasty, and she would give her right leg for a bottle of water.

The road started to curve to the right and as she came around the corner Dori was met with the most welcome sight. It appeared that Dori found herself outside of a small village. Quaint little thatched roof houses with smoke billowing out of brick chimneys. Tiny yards filled with garden beds and flowerpots, signs of life and almost no signs of danger.

The noise that had drawn her this way appeared to be a group of men working on what looked like the gate into town. Upon closer inspection Dori spotted a total of four men. Three of them almost looked identical. Sour frowns graced their round faces, they had noses that pointed up as if they had spent a lifetime looking down on others, and beady eyes completed the look. Each man had his own version of a greased-back hair style. Their clothes looked rather important and well kept; suits on each of them. Each suit a different colour of the rainbow.

One wore a ruby red suit jacket, pants, and bow tie to match. The man beside him wore a canary yellow suit in a similar style, and the suit on the third man was as purple as any quality plum. Though beautiful suits couldn't hide how out of shape these men were, with their bellies hanging over their belts a little much and the seams on their clothing slightly bulging.

All three men were shouting very rude things at the fourth man. The snap of their voices grated on Dori's nerves, running up and down her spine. These were by no means kind men and Dori had to be sure she proceeded with caution.

Getting closer Dori finally got a better look at the fourth man. He was easily a head taller than these three and had a completely different look to him. Sandy blonde hair just long enough to get in his eyes every time he swung his hammer. His arms glistened with sweat from the exertion, and yet it didn't seem like he would be taking a break any time soon.

His clothes were in far worse condition than his three companions. His shirt was a faded blue, almost as if the sun itself had stolen the vibrancy of it, making it old and worn with a few small holes forming around the seams. His grey pants were much in the same condition, with dull colour and a few raggedy patches sewn onto the knees.

"You call that quality work? My great aunt could do a better job on her death bed, and she was blind!" One of his counterparts shouted at him. The man looked back, and his honey eyes sparkled in the small amount of sun that came through. The look on his face was one of hurt and misunderstanding, as if he wasn't sure why his companions were spewing this hate at him. Companions that had pulled a picnic basket out of nowhere with exactly three chairs to recline in.

The basket appeared to be full of lush, rich food and frosty bottles of liquid, but not one of those men offered the tall man any refreshments at all, despite the fact that he openly stared at the basket like a man in the desert stared at a watering hole. His dry and cracked lips were a sign of just how parched he truly was.

"What the hell do you think you're looking at? Get back to work! We don't pay you our good money for you to waste your time daydreaming. That's what's wrong with you, what's been wrong with you since day one, your head is stuck up in the clouds! Ungrateful!" The one in plum snapped at his friend.

"After all that we've done for you, put a roof over your head and gave you plenty of clothing to keep you warm, this is how you treat us! With shoddy workmanship and no thought on how slowing down your work to daydream would affect all of us in town!" His yellow suited friend joined in the vicious words.

"If you don't get this gate fixed up before the end of today then anyone can enter our town! If any harm befalls a citizen because you couldn't work fast enough to keep us all safe, then it'll be your head on a pike in the morning! Get back to work!" Not to be outdone, the third man, in the ruby red suit, piped up.

Dori stood there in shock at the vile things these men easily spat towards their friend.

Here these ungrateful little weasels were sitting on their asses, watching this poor man work himself to the bone! The least they could do was offer him a drink to replenish some of the liquids he was sweating out!

But instead of standing up for himself the fourth man merely cowered, lowered his head, hunched his shoulders, and turned around to go back to work. A moment later the pit of a peach hit him in the back of the head.

"Hey! We're talking to you! Don't you ignore us! Turn around!"

The man turned with an apology written all over his face, when his eyes caught Dori's and surprise at another person on the road stopped him in his tracks.

"Here we go again, lost in a daydream! Hey, stupid! Are you even listening to us? What are you gawking at?" With that all three vicious men turned to see Dori standing there and each reaction was different.

The man in yellow sneered what she was sure he thought was a charming smile in her direction and raised his eyebrows, as if to say he was interested.

The man purple wiped his mouth on his sleeve, cleaning off any peach juice that may have run down his chin before using both of his hands to adjust his belt, lifting it back up over his extended belly.

The man in red looked at her with contempt and very little patience. His mouth turned further down in a permanent frown; he said nothing but the stare he was giving her said everything. She was not welcome here.

The only spot of kindness in the entire group came from the man holding the hammer, for he offered her a small, somewhat hidden, but very real smile.

Chapter 3

At a loss for what else to do, Dori gave a small wave at the men staring at her and a smile to the other man. Unable to look away from the kind eyes that had latched on to her own, Dori found herself moving in his direction until she was standing right in front of him, much to the chagrin of the other men he was with. All three started talking at the same time, spitting out their words at her.

"Keep moving, girlie, you're distracting the help!" The man in red motioned with his hands, trying to shoo her away as if she was nothing more than a pest or wild animal.

"Well, hello there." The man in yellow licked his discoloured lips as he opened his arms to her, as if he was offering her a valuable gift. His actions sent shudders down her spine.

"What's this? A common whore on the Enchantress's Road? You lot are supposed to stick to the shadows during the day … a few moments of your time and I won't let anyone know you were here." The man in purple kept adjusting his pants in a lewd gesture while looking her up and down. Honestly, all three of them made her stomach turn.

"Hello ... wait, did you just call me a whore?" Dori was taken aback at the insult, at the leering, and the general unpleasantness of the group. She wasn't expecting roses thrown at her feet, but perhaps just some kindness, or a friendly hello would have been a better response.

"Well, if the trashy clothes fit ..." The man in purple had moved to circle her as he was looking her up and down and the man in red kept sniffing in her direction. Dori became aware of how different her clothing choices must have looked to these men, especially since she was still in her pajamas and muck boots, but still, Dori's eyes widened as she couldn't believe the audacity falling out of their mouths.

Almost immediately her body became defensive, and she was made quite aware of just how out of sorts she was in this place. Searching for an ounce of friendliness Dori's eyes found the fourth man again, who had stood there smiling at her, as if he hadn't heard the cruel words spoken to her. The eye contact seemed to have spooked him out of whatever trance his was in, and he started to come to her defence.

"Now, fellas, let's not assume we know what this young lady is doing on the Enchantress's Road." He turned his attention back to Dori.

"I'm sorry for my companions, miss, it's just we aren't used to seeing anyone else out here and I'm sure they are just in a state of shock." He tried to explain to her but was cut off when the three men scoffed at his apology.

"Excuse me, are you speaking for us?" the man in red spat at him.

"Correcting us is more like it ..." the man in plum muttered to his friends in a snide tone.

"After all we've done for your moronic life, you think you get to correct us like this, in front of a stranger. A whore, nonetheless?" Almost instantly the three men turned from Dori and started to verbally attack one of their own. Immediately the fourth man raised his hands in defence and started backing up.

"Oh, I meant nothing by it, fellas, that's for sure. I just wanted this young lady to know we mean no harm to her. That she spooked us by showing up out of nowhere. But I would never assume to speak for you, or on your behalf as it were." He was practically tripping over his own words in an effort to apologize to these three louts.

"Bollocks! You know, all we've gotten from you is trouble and a lack of a decent work ethic. I've had just about enough of you!" The man in red stamped his feet as he spoke, as if he was a toddler throwing a tantrum.

"What do you suggest we do, brother?" the man in yellow inquired as he sneered both at her and the kind one, rubbing his hands together.

"I say we report him to the crown as a traitor. As someone who speaks half truths and who dares speak for those above his station in life. I say we bring him in and let the Enchantress decide just what kind of punishment is befitting him." The man in plum started raising his voice with every idea that fell out of his mouth.

Punishment for trying to be nice to a stranger, a stranger that was obviously lost––what kind of place had she found herself in? Dori couldn't just let this man get in trouble for trying to be nice to her. She had to speak up, to say something, anything, in his defence. Dori stepped closer to the angry men, her voice slightly trembling, but her courage pushing her to say it anyway.

"Now wait just a minute, he was just trying to be kind to me, is that so terrible?" The kind mans eyes snapped to her in shock, as if he had never been defended before by a stranger. The angry men flipped their attention to just her and she could feel the revulsion sliding down her spine, but still she stood tall.

"Shut your mouth, filthy whore! No one asked for your opinion." The man in yellow slapped Dori across the face and all the air seemed to be sucked out of her lungs. What was happening? This was completely unacceptable! How could they treat her like this? Anger welled up inside of her, but common sense took the lead as Dori shoved the anger down, fully aware that she was outnumbered and lost. A growl rose up from beside her, where the kind man stood.

"I wouldn't do that again if I were you …" The voice that came out of the fourth man was unlike any voice she had heard up to this point. The kind meekness had faded out and a dark undercurrent seemed to be leaching out of him. Dori looked up at him and saw his entire demeanor change. The other three men didn't seem to notice as much, as they kept chirping insults at him. They even went as far as to start throwing their leftover food at him, trying to reign him in. His once almost-goofy stance had straightened out, and the hammer he appeared to lightly hold was now clenched in his left hand, almost shaking with rage.

"Do not lay another hand on this poor girl." Using his hammer to point at the three goons, the man took a step to put himself in between Dori and her attackers. The three men hissed at him for daring to get in their way.

"Or what? Full of attitude this one, watch your step or to the dungeons you'll go!" The man in yellow started shaking his fist at the duo.

Dori started feeling more than unsafe and looked around for an exit. Unfortunately, she was surrounded on three sides and the only opening was where she came from. Not really wanting to go back into the forest alone, Dori tried calming everyone down.

"Let's all take a step back and maybe a deep breath. I'll just be on my way and you all can get back to your project. I'm sorry for the intrusion." Holding her hands up, as if talking to wild animals, Dori tried to walk around the man in yellow. He reached a grubby hand out and wrapped it around her bicep. It was there for mere seconds before a hammer came crashing down on the wrist bone holding her in place, shattering it and sending the man down to his knees in pain. Everything seemed to have exploded at once. The other two men advanced on her as if it was her fault but before they could get close a large, warm hand pulled her back and placed her, once again, behind the man with the hammer.

"You should have listened." The man with the hammer looked like he almost couldn't believe it himself. He had spoke up, stood up for her, and defended a stranger without second thought. It took about a minute for what he did to register in his own brain, and while it was computing, it was like his body took control and kept swinging the hammer to keep the other two away from them. The man in yellow rolled around on the ground, holding his wrist, shouting in vast amounts of pain.

"Look at what you've done, you lousy moronic piece of nothing! You broke my wrist!" The other two stepped in front of their friend, spit flying from their mouths as the insults and threats kept spewing out.

"They'll hang you for this for sure! You won't be alive to see tomorrow when the Enchantress hears about what you've done to one of her favorite cousins!" The face of the man in purple started mirroring the colour of his outfit, as his anger took control.

"The Enchantress will have to wait her turn, we're going to tear you limb from limb for this and then make you watch as we beat that little friend of yours to a bloody pulp! No one will dare give her an ounce of money! No one will recognize her when we're finished with her, and it'll be all your fault!" The man in red was infuriated at the thought of someone below them lashing out.

The horror started filling out the man with the hammers face as he started to realize what he had done. He didn't know what had spurred him on to act like that. These men have never treated anyone with kindness, so why did he destroy his entire life for this woman, this stranger?

A simple apology wouldn't be enough to make up for what he did. They were going to hang him in the gallows, for it was a capital offense to act out in a physical way, well in anyway, against members of the royal court. And yet it was as if his body was waking from a dream, and he knew without a doubt that he would go down swinging if it meant the lady pressed up against his back was able to make a run for safety.

"Please, he was just defending me. He didn't mean to hurt you. Please, this was all my fault!" Dori's voice was getting lost in a sea of hate, but that didn't mean the men forgot about her.

"Don't worry, girlie, we'll make you pay extra for what you've cost us today. Before we beat you bloody, we'll get a look at those whoring skills of yours. Might as well get what we can out of you before you're too broken to service anyone." A cold chill zipped through Dori's body. These men were going to attack her. They were going to rape her and beat her. Where the hell had she woken up?

The oddest feeling started coming off the man in front of her. His body seemed to start humming after that last threat. His eyes went dark as he focused all his ire on the man making the threats, the man in red.

Without so much as a warning he struck out, swinging his hammer at that man's knees, successfully breaking both in one swing. There was only one left standing. The man in purple noticed how the tides had started to turn, and so he turned his own body and started running. The man with the hammer carefully stepped away from Dori and started swinging his arm with the hammer around. He waited a moment and let go, watching his hammer fly through the air and into the back of the man in purple, who immediately fell to the ground, hit his head on a rock, and became unconscious.

"There is nowhere you can go that we won't find you. You made a mistake here. You never should have raised a hand against us. You just signed your death warrant," the man in yellow coughed at them, spit flying out of his mouth as he struggled to sit up with one broken wrist.

"Guess we better start running then." The kind man took her hand, walked by the man in yellow, giving him a swift punch in the face, and then pulled Dori with him at a run down the road.

It all seemed a bit absurd; this man didn't even know who she was. She didn't know a thing about him either and yet, standing beside him was the safest she had felt since she woke up in this terrible place.

"I'm Dori by the way," she huffed as she ran along side him. He glanced over at her with the sweetest look on his face, as if her name was precious to him. But it then occurred to him ...

"I'm ... I'm ... you know, I have no idea what my name is. They called me East."

Chapter 4

Dori and East spent what must have been a good hour running and looking behind them for any sign that they were being chased. But nothing seemed out of the ordinary. The roads were vacant, aside from the rare crow, which seemed like a blessing. However, East knew well enough that even letting a crow see where you were running to was dangerous, for they were messengers of the Enchantress. They would report back to her if they saw someone breaking her laws, and attacking the munchkies was against the law.

    Dori was still holding East's hand, and the more she thought about it the more she realized that, even though she had just witnessed a very violent outburst and possibly a personality disorder of some sort, she didn't feel any fear towards him. If anything, she felt a sense of belonging and safety. An air of familiarity floated between the two and Dori didn't really know how to feel about that. Watching him constantly turn around to watch the road they came from let Dori know that, despite appearances, they weren't safe.

"They called me East." His voice pulled her out of her inner ponderings, only to give her one more to wonder about. That phrase, 'they call me East', kept rolling around in her head. How did this man not know what his name was? What else didn't he know? He seemed to have some sense still, pulling her down roads that seemed familiar to him, but how far would his knowledge go?

When she'd first walked up to the group it had looked like they were a group of friends working on a project together, but looking back on it now it was clear that they were the employers, and he was their only worker. Worker, or slave, she had yet to figure that part out. Why it took three of them to keep him on task, considering how docile he seemed, was another confusing thought.

And what was this talk of the Enchantress, and the Enchantress's Road? Where did she end up? This road looked like nothing she had ever seen, old yellow brick that was crusted with dirt and weeds. In her experience, when royalty claimed something, like a road or a passageway, it was well taken care of by the crown. That didn't seem to be the case here.

Thinking back on those men acting in such a strange and terrifying way made Dori's head spin. She really was lucky that East had been with them. The thought of what may have happened if he wasn't there made her spine stiffen and bile climb her throat. While they may have been out of shape, three of them would have overpowered her.

Plus, the vile filth that they spit at her, the acts that they threatened, if East hadn't had been there it could have turned into a very dark situation very quickly. Dori was very aware that the man beside her was the only reason she was making a getaway. The man with no memory and, apparently, an easily triggered temper.

Dori took a moment to really look at East as he led her away from danger. His eyes looked terrified, and he looked behind them more than she did. Yet there was something inside of him that couldn't allow those men to hurt her, a perfect stranger.

It didn't make sense to Dori. They were treating him like garbage, and he seemed perfectly okay with it. He wasn't fighting back, not even when they threw food at him. What was it that caused him to cross the line, to physically attack them?

"I have no idea." His voice startled her, and she was now unsure if she had spoken any of her thoughts out loud. Confused, she looked up at him.

"Your face shows the world everything you're thinking. I can read you like a book. You're wondering what it was that caused me to defend you against my own employers to the extent that I did. Especially with you being a perfect stranger and those men being the only thing keeping me out of the dungeons. And the answer is, I don't know." East stopped moving for a minute, his stare drifting off into the forest that now surrounded them. They had gone far enough that the town they came from was behind them, and in front of them was nothing but wilderness and that damned yellow brick road.

"For as long as I can remember I have worked for those three men. I have let them treat me horribly. They call me names, they feed me only their leftover and spoiled food, and they give me nothing but jobs to do--the toughest work and they expect me to finish it in a timely manner." His voice held a sadness to it as he thought back on his past.

She couldn't believe what she was hearing. Dori couldn't imagine allowing anyone to treat her that way. East clearly could take them on physically, so what was it that held him back? What was it that made him the perfect timid worker? Dori didn't want to push him, especially since she couldn't find the words to comfort him. Anything she thought of didn't quite sound right. East scanned the horizon before setting his gaze on her.

"And up until you walked down that road and looked me in the eyes, I didn't think that there was anything wrong with the way they treated me." His voice took on a gravely tone, as if it hurt him to admit these things out loud. Emotion clogged his throat and tears filled his eyes. He looked away quickly to dab them away with his sleeve, almost ashamed that he was letting the emotions get to him.

"They made you eat spoiled food?" she asked in a quiet tone. Dori couldn't imagine living such a life. She put her hand on his arm, the only way she could think to show him support without overwhelming him. He took a deep breath, composed himself, and continued.

"It was like I was living in a fog and you coming down that road was like a gust of wind that blew it away. Standing there, listening to them say those vile things to you, I couldn't understand what I was doing there. And then he reached out and grabbed your arm." East had to take a controlled breath as his eyes landed on her arm and the anger in him bubbled up until it took control of his body. All his muscles strained, making it look like it had taken great effort to hold back from doing what he'd really wanted to do to those men. Dori put every ounce of energy into not rubbing the sore spot from where she was grabbed. It was unnecessary at this point to add fuel to the fire.

"Thank you for that, by the way. I don't want to think about what would have happened if we didn't get out of there." Dori's own voice started betraying her calm facade, as she squeaked out those last few words. East took a step towards her and gently grasped her chin in his rough hand. He stooped his neck until he was looking her in the eyes. The swirl of emotions he hid in them almost took her breath away.

"I know what would have happened. I've seen it before, and I did nothing. But not this time. Not you. They aren't allowed to have you like that." East ground the words despite the confusion in his gaze. For a moment they stood there, two strangers who, up until a few hours ago, didn't even know the other existed. Their fates were now intertwined in one of the most serious ways they could be. After a beat, East dropped his hand but kept her gaze.

"It's an odd feeling, not being able to remember how I came to be in their company. Not being able to remember much at all. It worries me, because if I've forgotten myself, then who else have I forgotten?" The wind started to pick up a bit and there was the scent of chopped wood and smoke from a campfire mixed with it. Dori could hear the regret in his voice, regret for forgetting a life that must have been more enjoyable than this one. Regret for forgetting anyone that he had cared about. Regret for not fighting for his own future, at least not until Dori appeared.

"We don't have to talk about if you don't want to. If it's too painful a topic we can come back to it at a different time." Dori didn't want to push East past his comfort zone. These conversations were important, but they were heavy and the day itself was already weighing on both of them.

"It is painful, but it's the strangest thing, Dori. Ever since you walked out of the forest all I seem to want to do is talk to you. Tell you all my most secret thoughts, those that I can remember anyway. Why is that? Who are you really?" East looked her in the eyes and a combination of curiosity and determination swirled in his irises. It was like he was trying to figure out the whole puzzle but, for whatever reason, he was only given half the pieces. Dori didn't know if now was a good time to tell him that she had no answers; that she, herself, was a bit of a puzzle. Maybe that was also a conversation for a different time.

"Just someone who is lost and looking for my way home." Taking a breath, she decided to keep it simple, at least for now. They needed to prioritize a few things, like a safe place to spend the night before the sun went down, and maybe something to eat to restore their energy. After those things were taken care of, she would tell him everything.

Just as Dori was about to tell East that they should get off the road and find somewhere safe, she tripped over a rock and fell to the ground. As she flung her arms out to catch herself the crystal that she had been grasping in her fist all morning went flying a few feet and landed in front of the duo. It looked completely out of place on the worn yellow brick, and it was as if the gem itself almost started whispering to their surroundings. The forest went quiet, the birds stopped singing, and even the wind stopped pushing the leaves around just to hear what the gem had to say.

It was almost as if time had stopped, and they were only able to move in slow motion. East couldn't believe it; he couldn't take his eyes off the crystal. His eyebrows knit together, and his mouth hung open. Dori looked up at him, feeling embarrassed and almost ashamed that she had hidden the beautiful rock up until this point. Realistically she had nothing to be ashamed of. This gem fell from the sky in front of her house, she didn't sneak off into someone's collection and steal it. And yet Dori felt shame redden her cheeks when she saw East's reaction.

"Where in the seven hells did you get that?" East didn't move an inch, didn't take his eyes off the of crystal, and almost didn't breathe as he waited for her answer. Dori was able to gather herself a bit quicker, dusting her clothes off as she stood up. This couldn't wait anymore, she had to at least tell him part of the truth.

"I found it outside of my home." Her voice wavering as she tried to gauge his reaction to see if he would turn explosive again.

"You said you weren't from around here and that gem is very much from around here, so don't you lie to me. Where did you get that?" The ease of his voice was gone, and East sounded as serious as he did when those men threatened her. Dori took a tiny step back involuntarily as East shifted his gaze onto her, a slight madness now reflecting in his eyes.

"I'm not lying, I promise I'm telling the truth. I found it outside of my house. It … uh … kind of just fell from the sky …" Dori was prepared for East to tell her she was crazy, to tell her she was a thief. She was aware of how it sounded. Even Dori had trouble believing everything that she had experienced in the last twenty-four hours. But all she had to offer him was the truth, in hopes that he could look into her eyes and see her good intentions. What she wasn't prepared for was the absolute flame of hope that lit up his eyes.

"That's impossible." His voice came out as barely a whisper as he stared at her in awe. Out of nowhere East started to grasp his head as if he was in terrible pain, his hands covering his ears and his face going white as if all the blood was draining from it. He started shouting out, screaming as if his head was on fire.

"What's happening, what's wrong?" Dori was trying to grab his hand, trying to calm him to understand what he was shouting about. All he could do was remove his left hand from his left ear and point to the crystal. Hoping she was interpreting him correctly Dori ran over to the crystal and brought it to him. She held it out to him, as if it was that easy to part with it. As if she didn't feel a chill go down her spine as she tried to give it away. Without touching it East used his left hand to guide the hand Dori held the gem in into her pocket, putting the crystal once more out of his sight. The gem felt warm in her hand and the chill that went down her spine was lifted. East had fallen to his knees, but his screaming had stopped.

It took a few moments before the pain started to ease out of his face and Dori took that chance to help East get to his feet so that she could usher him over to a log just off the road. With a whisper she asked him,

"East, what was that? What happened?" Her fingers turning the crystal over and over in her pocket. The forest around them had sprung back to life, the birds chirping and the leaves twirling in the wind once more, not that either of them took notice. Dori warily sat beside him and gingerly as she could. East set his hands down from his face and placed them on his lap as he tried to stop them from shaking.

"That was a memory resurfacing. At least that's what it felt like." His voice was once again husky. What kind of memory could have caused such a reaction? And what was it that brought the memory back? Was it simply seeing them gem or was there something more to it that she just didn't know about? It bothered Dori, not having any of the answers.

She looked him over for a minute, evaluating him and searching for any type of answer. Dust and dirt coated his face, his arms, and his hands. His hair was wild and unkempt, and his skin had the glow of someone who worked outside daily. His eyes, however, told the story of a man who was heartbroken, and his mouth told the story of someone who hadn't had much of a reason to smile for far to long.

From a distance he looked a bit raggedy, like he needed a washing up, but to Dori, however, he smelled the way a field does as the sun goes down. Warm earth and evening dew on the grass. Dori couldn't think of a more comforting smell. He smelled like summer. She needed to know more about him. Dori needed answers and she didn't think they could wait much longer.

"What was the memory?" Feeling bad for asking, Dori had to remind herself that without questions they weren't going to get anywhere. He was fully able to tell her if she was crossing a line, and if he did, in fact, want her to back off she would. At least for a bit. She owed him that much after showing up and completely flipping his world upside down. East visibly swallowed before answering her.

"Pain, heartache, absolute terror. And that bloody crystal." It was clear to Dori that he was holding something back, but she didn't want to push him at this point. The shaking had finally subsided in his arms and legs and the color had come back to his face.

"What does it mean for now? Do you need to go a separate way? Do you need to leave me?" Her voice betrayed her and the fear that she felt at the thought of once again being alone on her travels in a strange land leeched through. East snapped his head her way and looked at her as if she had grown a second head.

"Leave you? Now? After this? Absolutely not. If nothing else, it shows me that I need to stick to you like glue. We don't go anywhere without each other." Relief flooded her system. The two of them sat there, in the quiet for a few moments. Dori waited for as long as she could and then decided that they weren't safe so close to the road. Not if someone was hunting them down. And there was no way they weren't wanted after what had happened.

"Okay. But what direction do we go in from here?" She asked him.

East looked around at where they were and discovered that they were at a literal crossroad. Other than the way they came, there was three options to continue their journey. Each way looked identical to Dori, she would have to trust in East's knowledge of the land, that is if he could remember much of it.

"I know where we need to go. I need to find an old friend." The words came out slowly and East looked a bit confused; the look on Dori's face didn't look much different. The man who couldn't remember who he was remembered that he had friends? It was as if, once again, East could read her thoughts right off her face.

"Didn't know I had friends, that's new information." With a small, forced laugh he gave her a smile and in that smile, Dori saw enough of his character to know that she could trust him.

With so much time wasted already, Dori stood up, pulling East up with her slowly, making sure he was steady. She went to dust off her pajamas, which reminded her just how odd her clothing was.

"Okay, where is this friend of yours? And do you think he would have something better for me to change into, maybe something that could help me blend in a bit more." East looked her up and down, as if just noticing that she didn't really match their surroundings, and then he looked straight ahead, to the left, and then to the right. His long arm reached out and pointed to the road going left.

"That way. We go that way." And just like that the two of them were off once again.

Chapter 5

The pair had started walking in silence, both battling different thoughts in their heads. Dori kept turning the crystal in her pocket, trying to figure out what this crystal was. Obviously from East's reaction, it wasn't as simple as a rock falling from the sky, not that a rock randomly falling from the sky was simple. But there was a power to it. With her hand constantly wrapped around it in her pocket she could almost feel the energy surrounding the crystal vibrating against her skin.

And what importance did it hold for East? How did it find its way to her if it was from this land, this land that must have been far from her own. The more she thought about it the more questions she had. Looking over she could see the same type of confusion on East's face as he bunched his brows and chewed on his lip.

The road seemed to go on forever, and just when Dori wanted to ask how much further it appeared the road started to bend and curve into a forest. In the distance she could see some type of house starting to form. The fog was starting to rise around them like a blanket as the sun started to set, and Dori wasn't sure if it was keeping something hidden or if it was hiding them from something else.

Suddenly a small object whizzed past her ear and exploded on the tree trunk behind her. Both East and her flinched and ducked, when another object exploded on the road directly in front of them. Someone was shooting at them! How anyone could see in this fog, let alone shoot at moving targets, was beyond her comprehension. Once again, her life was in danger, and it hadn't even been a full day in this new land. Dori needed an exit strategy, and fast.

"Shit, quick! This way!" East took her hand and pulled her off the road and into the forest. Each shot that exploded around them had Dori flinching, but East wouldn't let her stop running. It occurred to her that East was navigating them as if he too could see through this fog. Was she the only one that couldn't see five feet in front of her face?

"What's happening?" Dori shouted over the adrenaline pumping in her ears. Every time she inhaled the fog a coldness seeped throughout her lungs, causing her to cough as if it were smoke she was inhaling.

"He's not expecting company." East didn't seem quite as panicked as she did, almost as if this was something he had been through before. His voice was calm, and he was acting as their lives weren't in danger.

"What? Who isn't?" Dori screeched. Her legs were getting tired from this latest sprint, and her feet started dragging. She was thankful East was holding her hand and pulling her along, or she would have tripped and fallen almost immediately.

"Don't worry, he'll stop eventually!" East kept zig-zagging her through the forest, hiding behind trees and ducking down every time a shot went off.

"Don't worry? Are you crazy? We are being shot at! What makes you think we shouldn't worry?" Another shot exploded just behind her head and Dori screamed.

"Because he's my friend!" East, who was practically yelling just so Dori could hear him over her own screams, pulled her down behind an old, fallen tree trunk. The trunk in question started getting hammered with flying bullets as wood and splinters started flying around their heads.

"If he's your friend then why is he shooting at us?" Dori ducked every time she heard a shot land near them. East, looking only a bit more relaxed than Dori at this point, even started flinching every time a bullet got close.

"He can be a little cranky. Look, no one is perfect!" Standing up for a friend that he didn't remember hours ago, East was something else, that was for sure. Dori was just going to have to go with him on this one for now.

"Okay, well, how do we get him to stop?" Dori's voice was becoming hoarse from shouting. East looked at her and thought about that for a second before giving her a troublesome grin and leaping out of their hiding spot. Dori tried to grab him to pull him back, but he was just out of her reach.

"Hey! It's me! It's me, man!" East started raising his hands and yelling towards where the bullets came from. One or two whipped by his head before silence enveloped them. Dori checked her own body, and when she didn't see any injuries or blood, she peeked around the log to make sure East was alright. Still standing with no wounds in sight, East looked just as relieved that the shooting stopped. He turned to her and bestowed upon her a full out grin. It was as bright as the sunrise over a wheat field.

"I think it worked." While his smile was contagious at this point, Dori wanted to smack that smirk off him for scaring her like that. Who just jumped into view while being shot at, hoping it would stop the bullets? Maybe Dori shouldn't have felt so safe with him. He may have been even crazier than she was.

"East?" A hoarse voice full of disbelief came from the direction of the house. East's face lit up even more, if that was possible, when he heard it. He took off running towards the house, all the while trying to gesture to her, telling her to follow him.

Dori took three deep breaths before slowly crawling out from behind the rock just in time to see a slightly taller and gruffer looking man step out of the house, with a shot gun in his left hand. East went barrelling towards him like a golden retriever finding his lost human. East flung himself at his friend as if they hadn't seen each other in decades. His friend embraced him with the same excitement and, from afar, it was a touching reunion to watch. As she got closer to the two, she could hear their hushed conversation.

"What the hell are you doing here, man? Do they know you're here? Does she?" The man used his free arm to embrace East once more before holding him at arm's length, looking for answers.

"I'm here with my new friend." East gestured towards Dori and for the first time the angry man pinned his eyes on her, stopping her dead in her tracks. When Dori first saw East, she could see the friendliness and kindness in his eyes. The way he held himself when she walked up had her feeling like she could trust him with her life from the very first moment they met. This man possessed zero of that allure, and Dori wasn't confident that he wouldn't still shoot her in an instant.

He was slightly shorter than East, but not by much. However, where East had more of a slim build, this man was stockier in the arms and shoulders. His short, dark hair was tussled and had a slight wave to it. The contrast of his ice-blue eyes and his tanned skin was almost breathtaking. His attitude, however, left a lot to be desired.

"Who the hell is that?" He sounded offended and disgusted, his face scrunching up like she was a puzzle he was annoyed he would have to figure out. East looked slightly embarrassed at the way his friend addressed her and shuffled his feet back and forth a bit.

"Language, please, North. We're in the presence of a lady." East gave her a small grin, hoping to ease any tension she was feeling. Dori almost snorted at that. Out of all the things she was offended by right now, a little foul language was the least of her worries. Especially if this guy was willing to use his guns to protect them. North merely rolled his eyes at his friend and pretended he didn't hear a thing East said. Instead, North turned his defensive set of questions towards Dori.

"Well, who the hell are you? What did you do to him, why is he not at his workstation?" North kept advancing towards her until he was within inches of her face. Despite his off-putting behaviour around guests, his scent worked at calming Dori, almost as if it was designed to lower her own shields and keep her off-guard.

It took everything in her to not back up, but Dori was tired of being pushed around. Before she could say anything, East was putting himself between the two of them, once again putting Dori behind him for her protection. Only this time his hands were up, and palms were open, a gesture showing that he meant nothing by it.

"They weren't very nice to me at that place, man, I didn't want to be there anymore. Why can't I just work here, with you?" East was a grown man, and yet he sounded like how a teenager would, asking for something from a parent. Dori took that moment to look around the exterior of the house and noticed a large collection of giant wood carvings. There were wooden coatracks, wooden dressers, animals carved out of tree trunks. Everything looked exquisite. The detail on the animals was phenomenal.

"We've told you before, you can't stray like this. She won't like it. We must bring you back to your station before they come looking for you." That snapped Dori's attention back to the men in front of her. East's face looked defeated, as if he was a scolded puppy who'd chewed on the wrong slipper. She had to speak up.

"You can't send him back there, they were awful!" Her voice, still hoarse from all the yelling, crackled when she spoke. East pulled her beside him and put a hand on her back in appreciation for her speaking up. He looked back at North.

"She's right, they were never very nice to me. Besides, they won't accept me back." East looked at his feet as the memory of what he did came back to him. North noticed the difference in demeanour immediately.

"What do you mean they won't want you back ... what did you do?" If possible, this man looked even more furious, but he wasn't aiming his inquiry at East, he was aiming it at her. Dori blinked twice before she registered that he was expecting an answer.

"I ... I--uh ..." How was she going to explain that, because of her, his friend got fired from his job, possibly turned into a criminal, and was being hunted down by this Enchantress that they keep mentioning. East took off some of the pressure and got in North's face before Dori could say anything.

"She didn't do anything wrong. They did! They were going to hurt her, so I stopped them." Finally, a bit of pride appeared in his face and in his voice as he straightened his back and looked North in the eyes. Pride for standing up for what was right. North narrowed his eyes at East and stared him down.

"You stopped them how?" North's voice got eerily quiet as he started talking through his teeth. East visibly swallowed but kept his stature before continuing.

"Well, they wouldn't listen to reason, not that I know how to reason with others very well, so I did the only thing I could think of in that moment." His voice trailed off and North knew where this was going and already was shaking his head in disbelief.

"Tell me you didn't …" Instead of pure fury, there was actual concern in his voice as it turned softer. Concern for East and what the consequences may be for whatever he did. East took a step back and turned his attention to the horizon, not because he was looking for something outward, but more so he could focus on the memory of what occurred mere hours ago.

"It was an odd thing, almost as if my body had a mind of its own, which is the strangest thought to think, seeing as how there is only one mind in my body and it's my mind all the same." East started to speak in a way she hadn't heard before. It sounded like his brain was short circuiting and, while he knew what he was trying to relay to his buddy, he couldn't get the words coming out to make any sense. Watching him talk like that was like watching a person in the middle of a maze figure out which way to go. North didn't seem as intrigued by it; in fact, it was as if everything that East did annoyed him to no end.

"Lord, I forgot you had the jibber jabber thing going." North wiped at his eyes and forehead in frustration, but East didn't notice a thing and kept talking.

"So, there I was, standing between her and them, kind of like I'm standing now, only I don't think you're the threat that they were, not by a long shot." Now that things had settled down Dori could agree with that statement. At least, until North found out what happened, then Dori could see all bets being off. North cut him off.

"This could take forever. You, girl, tell me what happened." North was looking right at her. His eyes begging her to end whatever tangent East was going on. East kept talking, as if he didn't hear North at all.

"And my body just decided it was taking action. They were saying these heinous things and they made to advance on her, grabbed her like she was a bag of flour on a shelf, something to heave over their shoulders, whether or not the flour wanted to be heaved." Dori piped up the moment East had to take a breath.

"He saved me." Simple as that. No dramatic flare, no over sharing of details, just straight and to the point.

"I warned them, I did, but like someone with straw in their ears, they didn't want to listen. So, I hit them." Both North and Dori looked over to East at that statement. North with surprise and Dori with regret.

"You what?" North took another step towards East. He really wasn't going to like what else East had to say. Dori took a few steps back for self preservation.

"Multiple times. With my hammer." East kept answering like North wasn't getting more and more agitated as the conversation went on.

"Which one?" Did it matter?

"All of them. It sure did make them angry, but they wanted to hurt her so I made sure to hurt them first ... and that's when we decided we had to run and the only place I could think of that made me feel safe was here. So, we walked here. Oh, this is Dori." East looked over to her and leaned into his friend, whispering the last part.

"She has the thing." North scrunched his eyes closed. He looked like the father of a teenager who couldn't keep themselves out of trouble.

"You're an idiot." Dori couldn't tell if he was kidding the way that some friends do, but instinctually she couldn't let him talk like that. Especially after seeing how those other men would talk down to East.

"Hey, you don't need to speak to him like that!" North appreciated having someone else to vent his anger on, turning to Dori with a scowl painted across his face.

"Don't tell me how to talk to my friends, girl." Dismissively he turned back to East, ready to lecture him some more. Dori wasn't having it.

"Stop calling me girl, my name is Dori!" Waving her arms around Dori stepped in between North and East. If she wanted to be the one to fight it out with him, so be it.

"Okay, Dori. Do you realize what he did? What this means? Who will be coming after, not only you, but someone that means more to me than you'll ever understand? All because you couldn't take a couple good for nothing munchkies calling you bad names?" Everything he was saying came off with an air of condescension.

"First of all, what the hell is a munchkie? And secondly, it wasn't just names, they were going to hurt me, for just walking by at the wrong time. And the way they were treating him, it was wrong. You don't treat people like that, I wasn't going to just walk by and let it continue!" East smiled at her the simplest smile he had, but the most tenderhearted smile, as if the thought of someone standing up for him wasn't one he had often. North wasn't getting it though; whether it was intentional or not, he kept glossing over the fact that East did something to protect an innocent person.

"How bad did you hurt them? Can you apologize and maybe accept a punishment?" North was just not listening; did he have wool in his ears? His friend was suffering where he was at.

"He's not going back! Aren't you listening to the conditions he was left in? No one deserves that! It's like you're heartless or something!" Dori threw the statement out there without much thought, but it was enough to silence North for a minute. He almost flinched back when she said it, but quickly pulled himself together. His voice got lower, and he spoke a bit softer.

"Or something. Look, he doesn't have a choice. None of us do, you daft woman! Have you had your head in the sand for the last decade! Look around, this isn't the homeland that we all know and love."

East finally stepped in, cutting North off.

"That's what I'm trying to tell you. She's not from here!"

North took those words in and looked Dori up and down for the first time. The strange way she talked, not knowing the state of the country, and the outfit she was wearing. So many clues that he didn't notice at first.

"What do you mean by that?" Clearing his throat, he felt a small spark, so tiny he couldn't even properly describe it, light somewhere in his body. It was like a tickle at the back of his brain, a message was trying to get through to him, but he couldn't quite get it.

"I'm not from around here. I don't even know where here is." Dori was ready to just rip that band aid right off. No use in putting it off. Lack of information would only make this conversation go in more circles. They needed clarity, and fast. East only knew one way forward.

"Show him. Show him the thing in your pocket. North, man, you are not going to believe this. Not that I know what it means, but I do know it means something. Something important. That's why we came here. I knew you would know what to do with it. You would know what it was. Because my brain is broken." Both North and Dori stilled as East kept talking. They didn't know how aware East was during his ramblings or if he understood that no one really understood what he was saying. East took a breath and kept speaking his truth.

"It has been for a long time, so I don't know things anymore. But you do. I may be stupid, but that much I know. And you'll know the right thing to do here. You always have." There was a moment of silence as the two men looked at each other. Something passed through them that Dori couldn't quite understand. North barely nodded at his friend before looking at Dori.

"Show me. Girl." Dori raised her eyebrows at him. Respect should go both ways, so if he wanted answers and to see what she had, he was going to have to learn her name before they went any further. Annoyance flitted across his face as he realized she wouldn't answer him when addressed like that. Rolling his eyes he gave her what she wanted.

"Shit. Show me, Dori. Please." Pleased enough to be making progress with him, Dori stuck her hand in her pocket to pull out the crystal. The man turned to East before she could pull it out.

"You're not stupid. This isn't your fault." North put his hand on East's arm as they shared a quiet moment. East nodded once, looking down at his feet. The tension was becoming thick around them. The longer she was around them, the more Dori wanted to know what had happened here. Dori pulled the crystal out of her pocket and held it towards the man as if offering it up. He took a deep inhale with wide eyes.

"What the fuck! Where did you get that?!" North didn't dare touch it, he just stared at it as if it was a live snake that was getting ready to jump up and bite him.

"Language! I told you; it was something important. I was right, right?" If East was right and this thing in her hand was something of importance in this land, then how the hell did it find it's way to her front yard?

"It's something … it's … get inside, now. Both of you." The change in demeanor almost gave her whiplash. North started scanning the forest, as if they were surrounded by enemies, as he practically pushed her inside his cabin. Just as he shut the door Dori heard a screech in the distance, unlike anything she had ever heard before. On their journey here they barely saw more then a handful of birds, but Dori did remember the growl of something in the forest when she first woke up.

Mere seconds later something landed just outside the door, as if it dropped from the sky. It wasn't small though; no, it was something big. And it started hammering on the door with angry fists.

"Shit." North paled.

Chapter 6

For what felt like an eternity no one in the room moved and Dori was barely breathing. The pounding continued, getting more and more aggressive as it went on. The wooden door wouldn't be able to hang on much longer if whomever was on the outside really wanted to get in.

North jumped into action, shoving Dori into what could only be described as a small coat closet. His eyes looked wild, communicating without saying a word that she was to remain there, silent, if she wanted to come out of this alive. The door closed on her just as she saw East slipping into another closet down the hall. How he fit in it was a mystery, but somehow, he'd pretzeled himself inside without making an ounce of sound. Dori was mostly standing in the dark, except for the small slit of light coming through where the door didn't quite line up with the frame. From that spot she could see part of the front door.

The banging continued but North waited until he knew there was no sign of his visitors.

"Yeah, I'm coming! Settle yourselves down!" he shouted. Which was apparently the wrong thing to say as it seemed to only have enraged whoever was on the other side of the door.

"Open up by order of the Enchantress, before I knock your fuckin' teeth through your throat!" A deep, angry voice shouted.

North pulled the door open, and Dori had to swallow the scream that dared come out of her throat. Standing outside the door was possibly the most hideous creature she had ever seen. Things like that only existed in nightmares, and yet it stood, and it talked.

It looked like someone took a cross between a gorilla, a human, and sprinkled in a few bat genes to even things out. This creature filled the entire doorway, not including the wings that dragged behind it. He was big, he was bulky. His body was covered in dark, thick hair from, what she could see. He wore a military outfit with a patch on the left lapel that clearly read 'Enchantress's Reserves'. The muscles in his arms, all the way up to his neck, were flexing as if he was expecting trouble.

This creature merely pushed North out of the way as it came through the door. As he stepped inside, the floorboards beneath him let out creak after creak.

"What's going on here?" The beast's deep voice vibrated off the small entrance way as he started looking around, searching for something.

"What's going on here is that you're disturbing me for no reason and messing up my house." North gave off the appearance of someone annoyed and put out, and not someone hiding two fugitives in his home. Dori had to commend him for that. If it was her, she would be curled up in a ball, shaking with fear. The creature grunted at North before continuing to look around corners and under furniture.

"I never come around for no reason. Your buddy went missing from his workstation today, where he went on the attack and almost killed three of the Enchantress's cousins. Wouldn't happen to know anything about that, would you?" the creature grunted. North feigned shock as this monster turned to observe his reaction to the news.

"Knew nothing about that. Gee, that's terrible." North shrugged, knowing he wouldn't be able to push his attitude much farther.

"Hmm. So, you wouldn't happen to be hiding him around here, or anyone else?" Dori could hear the beast's footsteps walking around as he searched the house.

"As you can see, I'm here all by my lonesome. Who else are you looking for?" If North tried to keep the sarcasm out of his voice it didn't show.

"I don't answer your questions, you answer mine. You're telling me you haven't heard from him or seen him?" the creature snapped. The aggravation in his voice had Dori physically shaking. There would be no way out of this.

"No one has been around here for years." With a straight face full of forced confidence, North held his ground.

The creature walked right up to North, getting inches away from him. North, to his credit, barely blinked. If Dori didn't know any better, she would say North didn't even feel intimidated by this thing. The creature grunted a few more times.

"Why don't I believe you?" The hot breath from his nostrils fanned over North's face.

"I don't know, I have such a trustworthy appearance." North grunted back.

The creature grinned for a minute, letting the silence settle, before he took a swing, knocking North down with a punch to the face. Every muscle in Dori's body tensed. She wasn't sure how long East would allow his friend to be beaten, given how he reacted when someone tried to attack her.

The beast took another swing at North, who was now lying on the floor, blood coming from a cut on his lip. North, however, was barely defending himself, as if he knew the moment he tried fighting back things would go wrong. Dori wasn't sure how long she would be able to watch this beating. The guilt from being the reason North was getting beaten was starting to eat her up. This wouldn't be happening if they had kept going on the road. But instead, they brought trouble here.

It only took until the third hit before East couldn't hold back, and came flying out of the closet, fists swinging with a battle cry. The creature merely looked pleased as he ducked left and right, not allowing East to land his punches. North was up in an instant and tried stopping East.

"I knew I smelled moron. Hello, East." the creature smiled cruelly. North was now holding East back, both men breathing heavy.

"You aren't supposed to be here. That's a violation. And getting your buddy in trouble for lying for you. That's another violation. And you know what we do to people who violate our rules, now don't you?" The creature grinned, showing off his grotesque teeth.

"Get a hold of yourself, he just wants us to fight back so he has an excuse to end us." North kept pushing East back, willing his friend to listen.

"You don't *touch* my friends," East snarled past North.

"What's got you so upset there? You must know this isn't the first time I've stopped by to give North the beating he deserves. What has you so wound up this time?" The sneer this creature was displaying was enough to make anyone sick. Dori had to wonder though; did they know she was here?

"Rumour has it that while you were beating the Enchantress's cousins, you were defending a little minx that you found on the road. Where is she at? We have a few questions for her."

Dori shut her eyes and willed East to not say anything. She knew, though, that he was so worked up, he wasn't thinking straight.

"You leave her alone, I'll rip your fucking skull off of your fucking neck if you so much as breathe on her, you monkey bastard!" With every word he spoke East started shouting louder and louder, allowing his anger to take over.

North closed his eyes in defeat, knowing East played into the beast's hand perfectly. It wasn't fully his fault. He couldn't see the manipulation for what it was. It was in that moment that the creature knew his intuition was correct.

Dori's heart was hammering inside of her chest. It was a miracle that the three others in the entrance way couldn't hear it. Her palms were slick with sweat as she tried pushing herself as far back in the closet as possible. She couldn't blame East; he was outsmarted and that was something he couldn't control. Still, she had nowhere to run, nowhere to hide.

"Ah, so the rumours were correct. Where are you hiding her? If she's that important to you, you wouldn't have left her behind, would you? Hard to protect something that isn't close to you. And if you were hiding out here, it stands to reason that she's hiding somewhere here with you." The creature leaned in close as if trying to smell any lies coming off East.

The threat blanketed the room and East stopped moving. He finally understood the danger he was putting Dori in by simply trying to protect her. North caught East's gaze and held it, hoping it would stop East from looking directly at the closet that Dori was hiding in. He knew, however, that they would have to come up with a plan and quick. It was a small cottage. The Enchantress's guard would find Dori in under a minute if he really wanted to.

The creature started walking around, pushing furniture over, knocking things off shelves, making a show of looking for her. North stood completely still, refusing to even look anywhere but at East. He knew the moment one of them moved it would be a clue as to where she was hiding.

East was doing his best not to give anything away, but the creature knew how to push buttons. As he shifted closer to the closet that Dori was hiding in East involuntarily flinch forward an inch. It wasn't much, but it was enough. The creature smiled, knowing exactly where the girl was hiding.

"You boys best remember; the Enchantress always wins."

The creature knew how to play North, he knew how to play East, but what he didn't know was that when cornered and in danger, Dori became unpredictable. So, while he was lecturing the boys Dori was searching the closet for something to protect herself with.

The creature turned, flung the closet door open, and was immediately met with a well-sculpted lion's face, made from solid wood, as it smacked him in the face. The creature stepped back a few steps at the unexpected impact, allowing Dori to get out of the closet, where she reached for the coat rack, and with a strength she didn't know she possessed, lifted it up and smacked the creature across the back of the head with it, knocking him to his knees. Both North and East couldn't believe their eyes and it took them a moment to jump into action.

The creature didn't stay down long, and now he was pissed. Immediately he lunged for Dori but was met with East's fists. North quickly used one hand to undo the buckle on his his leather belt, tearing it out of his belt loops in one pull, and with the grace of a feline, he jumped on the creatures back, wrapping the leather around his throat, and proceeded to choke him.

While the creature was outnumbered, he was still twice the size of North and it took a few moments of struggling to even get him on his knees. The creature grabbed East's fists, using the momentum to bring East close enough to head butt him. It was like East's head met with a solid wall, knocking him to the ground while the room starting spinning for him.

The creature then grabbed North's arm from around his neck, pulling him over top of his head and throwing him to the floor. The creature pulled the belt off his own neck and wrapped it around North's.

"Not so tough now, are you?" he grunted, spit and sweat finding their way down to North's ear and the creature whispered in it. With East down and North in serious trouble, Dori kept looking around for something that could help.

"All this for some bitch? You dare dishonor the Enchantress for some piece of ass? I'm disappointed in you, North. No matter, we'll fix you and your friend up, disappear the girl, and then maybe you'll remember why we are the ones in power while you men can't even remember your fucking names."

That line caught Dori's attention. Did North also have troubles remembering things? Dori had to do something to help before she would be getting any answers.

Once again grabbing the first thing she could find, Dori picked up the wooden chair that sat beside the front door and proceeded to break it over top the creatures back. Instantly, with a deep growl, he let North go and turned to Dori. North rolled away, coughing and inhaling oxygen at an alarming rate. East was starting to get up, still a bit wobbly. Dori looked back at the creature just in time to see him lunge for her. He grabbed her by the throat and pushed her up against the wall.

"That wasn't very nice." The spit from his mouth flew out onto her cheek as Dori tried to free herself by scratching at the creature's arm and kicking at his legs, but he stayed standing strong. She couldn't breathe, she couldn't move. Tears started falling down her face as she attempted to call for help, but she couldn't even do that.

The creature got close to her face, close enough that his warm, earthy breath invaded her nose, almost causing her to vomit.

"Now, who the fuck are ..." A gurgle rose up from his throat as his words became stuck. The creature stilled even more, and blood started to fall from his mouth. Dori didn't understand what was happening at first, and it wasn't until the creature's grip let up and he fell to the ground that she saw East standing behind the creature, clutching a bloodied knife in his left hand and an equally bloody pair of shears in his right.

The creature struggled for mere moments before he was fully dead, and no one moved an inch until it was certain he wasn't coming back to life.

"Shit," North murmured. They all felt that this time.

Chapter 7

North was moving before Dori even caught her breath. He picked up an empty sack by the front entrance and started quickly placing items into it. A few pieces of clothing, a few apples from a small shelf, and what looked like a full waterskin. His deep voice echoed around the room.

"We've got to move. The Enchantress will notice her number one guy didn't make it back. They'll be here before night fall and we need to be very, very far away." He was talking straight to her, and Dori found herself nodding, like it made the most sense in the world to be going on the run with these two men. It hadn't even been an entire day and she was already a fugitive in another land, again. North looked her up and down before grabbing a few more items out of the closet and thrusting them into her arms.

"You can't keep wandering around looking like that, you look ridiculous." Trying not to be offended by that, Dori was appreciative of the clothes. She quickly went around the corner into what looked like the bedroom and changed into North's clothes. The dark grey pants were far too long on her, but they felt like they would be warm. She rolled the cuffs up and then realized that she would need better footwear, staring down at her cold feet. A black long sleeve shirt was next, and as she placed it over her head, she realized how much it smelled like North. Dori picked up her old clothes and rolled them into a ball, not wanting to leave them behind.

As she was walking around the corner, out of the bedroom, North shoved a set of boots into her face.

"Here. They'll be big on you, but they will be warm. I shoved some extra socks in the toe to help a bit. If that doesn't work at least you'll have extra socks to wear." With that he looked over at East, who was still staring at the body on the floor.

"*East*! Snap out of it, now isn't the time. I need your help. East!" But East just stood there, staring down at the two well-placed wounds on the body in front of him. He didn't even know what to say about it. It was all instinct. He didn't know where he learned it or how he came to have this information, but he knew exactly where to stab the creature in the back to make sure he never got up again. Was this something else that the curse was hiding? Had he killed before? Dori passed North her crumpled up clothes and walked over to East.

"We should wash you up before we go." Her voice was a mere whisper, partly because her throat was on fire, and the other part because the situation called for a little caution.

East finally looked away from the body and into her eyes. Torment was reflected there; a broken man who was confused by the power his own hands held. He roughly swallowed, his voice coming out grated.

"I told him not to touch my friends. He didn't listen."

Dori nodded at him, approaching him with caution, her hands out like she was walking towards a feral animal and didn't want to frighten it.

"I know. There is no judgement here. You saved my life. Again." Dori told him.

North was keeping an eye on them while he went to the kitchen and threw what food and supplies he could find into a second sack. He felt for his friend; North knew the confusion he was going through, but they just didn't have time to go through it right here.

"Dori. Take East to the rain barrel outside to wash off his hands. We leave the moment he's clean." North had used her name to get her attention. Once he had her eye contact, he tried to convey to her just how thin of a line they were walking right now. East would listen to her, for whatever reason he had become her personal guard. If she said they had to go outside to wash him up, he would listen and follow her outside. North just hoped the cold water and fresh air shook East out of this daze.

Dori grabbed Easts hand and led him outside. The sun was going down faster than she would have liked. The rain barrel wasn't far from the door and East let Dori walk him right up to it. She rolled up both of his sleeves with care and placed his hands into the cool water. After waiting a second and seeing that he still needed some direction, Dori started using her fingers to rub the blood off his hands. East didn't say anything and didn't put up any fight. It was hard to tell if the cold water was affecting him at all. Dori's hands were starting to shake from the cold but his were completely still. His eyes were still empty as he kept them casted down.

Throughout the day Dori had seen many different versions of East. She saw him protective and confident; she saw him clueless and subservient, and when they found North, she got to see him relaxed and, well, a bit goofy. But this was something else all together. Traumatized and shutting down was by far the hardest version of East for Dori to see. All she wanted to do was hug him and tell him everything would be okay.

Dori was still standing with East, rubbing his hands with hers, when North came and stood beside her. He had three separate sacks with him that each looked full to the brim. Dori pulled her hands out of the water, shook them a few times, and then wiped them dry on her pants.

"Where do we go?" Dori asked North, knowing whatever the answer, it would be a place she had never heard of.

"We have another friend that I'd like to check in on. If the Enchantress thought to send someone here to me looking for East, then she definitely sent one his way. After we make sure he's okay we'll come up with a plan." North explained.

That seemed to spark something behind East's eyes.

"You think she went after West?" East pulled his hands out of the rain barrel before drying them on his pant legs. His eyes seemed clearer, as if he was coming back to himself. It didn't go unnoticed by Dori that his protectiveness over his friend was what snapped him out of it. East seemed to be led by protectiveness.

"There's a good chance. If she hasn't already, she will after she discovers what went on here." The sky was growing dark around them, and it was making North uncomfortable standing out in the open like this.

"We have to leave now, and we'll probably be walking most of the night." North stated while handing each of them a sack to carry.

"What's this?" Dori asked as she tried to swing it over her shoulder. The sack proved to be heavier than she thought, and it caused her to take a few steps backwards. North put his hand on her shoulder to steady her.

"Supplies. Bread. A waterskin. Few pieces of cheese." North swung the bag he was carrying over his shoulder and it clanked with metal. Dori just raised her brows at him, knowing water and food wouldn't make those noises. North glanced over at East before answering.

"Protection. Just in case." North declared.

East tensed, understanding what North meant and not wanting to touch another weapon any time soon. He turned and started walking down the road, back into the forest. This time it looked more ominous. Shadows danced all around it, and if it wasn't for the man that had killed to protect her, and the other man who would kill to protect the first, Dori was sure she would be running the other way. North followed East and Dori ran after them, not wanting to be left behind.

Chapter 8

A few hours down the road, the sun was completely down, making the road hard to see through the trees. A chill and mist in the air had Dori shaking, her legs getting tired, and her stomach grumbling. North looked back at her but didn't say anything. The only sound, other than the crickets and bugs, was their footsteps on the brick road. More than once Dori sent up a silent thank you to North for the improvement in footwear. While sore, her feet were no longer cold.

After a few more quiet moments of walking and shivering, East stopped and pulled her to the side. He took the sack from her and dropped it onto the road, placing his beside it. He then pulled off his top shirt and handed it to her. Dori wanted to protest, but who was she kidding, she was shaking like a leaf. Taking it and pulling it over her head Dori embraced the warmth that surrounded her immediately.

"We're not far. Once we get there, we can have something to eat and a small rest. Hang in there." East spoke to her gently as he picked both sacks back up, handing Dori hers. Dori smiled at him for the kindness.

North walked by them, grabbing Dori's sack right back out of her hands, and kept on walking. East shrugged at her and kept going. The mood swings from North were starting to make her dizzy. Did he like her? Was he merely putting up with her for East? She couldn't get a read on him, and it was starting to bother her. For now, she would put up with his moodiness, but when they found a place of safety, she would have to evaluate how safe she was with him, or how expendable she was to him.

When they reached their destination, Dori almost missed it in the dark. The small cottage looked as if it was being swallowed by the forest around them. Old leaves and twigs covered the roof, which looked like it had seen better days. The small porch had multiple little piles of rotting garbage, along with animal feces and debris. The windows looked smashed in, and the only door Dori could see was hanging off its hinges. The cabin looked like it had been through a tornado and then abandoned.

Dori watched as East and North walked around the perimeter, assessing what they were seeing and quietly talking back and forth. Dori didn't want to be left out of the conversation, so she walked towards them, her footsteps kicking up dust and leaves everywhere she walked.

"Are you sure this is where he lives?" Dori directed her question at North; he always seemed to have an answer for everything. He barely looked her way while trying to look inside the darkened cabin through one of the broken windows.

"Of course, I'm sure." North's gruff voice gave way to his annoyance at such a question. Dori didn't mean anything by it, but the place didn't look inhabitable at first glance.

"It's just, it doesn't look like anyone … or anything lives here. Maybe a few squirrels, but that's about it." Dori stated, trying her best not to come across as rude, especially since it was obvious that whomever they were looking for meant something to them. East walked up to the duo.

"Oh, I don't know, it looks ... lovely?" East said, giving her a small smile. He was trying to lighten the mood for her. Dori looked back at him in shock, going along with it just to see some lightness in his eyes.

"The roof is caving in! There are branches that have fallen on the house. Honestly, if you hadn't have walked us right to the front door, I wouldn't have even known this was a house." Dori squeaked at him.

North got in between them and ended their playful banter in such a way that only someone with his disposition could.

"Alright, enough chatter. He's here, somewhere. *West*! Where are you, man? Come on out!" North shouted. Dori jumped at the sudden volume and closeness. All three stood completely still with open ears, straining to hear anything resembling an answer. Silence was the reply.

"Do you think, maybe, we're scaring him?" Dori asked, figuring that this friend of theirs probably had his own demons working against him, especially if he went through the same traumatic event that both East and North seemed to have gone through. East gave her a sharp look, slightly offended.

"Scaring him? We're his friends. West! It's East! We need to talk, are you around?" East bellowed.

Again, they were greeted by silence. The only sound was that of the nocturnal insects in the forest and the slight wind rustling the old leaves covering the cottage. After waiting another moment North let out a harsh sigh.

"We don't have time for this. I'm going in." North grunted.

The leaves crunching under his heavy feet as he walked quickly to what was left of the front door. When North went to pull the door open the entire thing came off in his hand, to the surprise of all three. Dori had to smother the small giggle that threatened to come out of her at the sight of this overly gruff man holding a door in his hand with a clueless look on his face. He looked back at her, as if knowing the amusement it brought her.

"Oh, well, oops?" She blurted as she walked up to him and peeked into the cottage. The giggles stopped there when all she could see by the light of the moon was clutter. Clutter, covered in layers and layers of debris. Random items were stacked up against the wall, to the roof, which was, in fact, caving in at multiple different spots.

"Is it even safe to go in?" Dori asked, not sure they should be walking through a place with so many obvious safety concerns, especially in the dark of the night. East seemed to understand her hesitations better than North did.

"She's right. Even if we made a torch to light up the inside, we may just walk by an important clue that could tell us where he went or what happened to him." East stated.

North put the door down, leaning it against the wall right beside the door frame.

"What do you suggest then?" North may have been looking at Dori when he asked, but the question was directed at East, who slightly shrugged his shoulders while taking in everything else that was covering the porch.

"Well, we could clear a small area right here and take a rest. Dori needs to eat something or she's going to fall over, and I could use a bit of a sit down. The sun will be up in about an hour or so, and then we can start going inside to see what we can find." East explained.

Dori liked the sound of that plan, mostly because it came with food, and she would be able to get off her aching feet. North didn't seem quite as convinced.

"And what about the Enchantress's guards? What are we going to do if they show up out of nowhere and we are out in the open like this?" he asked, gesturing to the area that was supposed to be the front yard, but with the weeds and overgrown plants growing uncontrollably someone would have to walk right up to them to notice anyone was there.

"No offense, but looking at that door, what makes you think they haven't already been here? The leaves and garbage all make sense, but what kind of abandoned cottage has a door that looks like it's been bashed in. Someone did that, maybe recently." Dori replied.

North looked Dori over sharply before responding.

"Fine, we wait for first light. But get your rest while you can, princess, because come sunup we're on the move again." Not one for having to be told twice Dori helped East shuffle some of the piles aside, making enough room for three people to sit, leaning against the wall. A small worn broom fell from behind one of the piles and, despite it missing much of its thistle, Dori used it to sweep away any excess dirt from their new resting spot. It wasn't perfect, but it was something.

As the three of them sat down, Dori in the middle, the silence started to envelop them. East looked over at Dori, who, despite the extra shirt, was back to shaking and shivering, and threw his arm around her. There was nothing romantic about it, merely a person offering comfort and warmth to a member of his traveling party while they waited for the sun to come up.

North looked over at the two, slightly amazed at the reactions East was showing after only knowing this woman for less than a day. North may not have felt the same kind of protectiveness towards Dori, but he had to admit that the energy radiating off her was nothing but kind and good. It was the only reason he hadn't suggested ditching her back at his place. East had years of anything but kindness thrust upon him. Who was North to try and take this budding friendship away from him, especially given the sincerity that dripped from Dori's mouth every time she talked to him.

He wouldn't completely drop his guard around her, but North felt confident enough in their new companion that he closed his eyes for a few moments of rest, knowing it was safe enough to do so.

Dori didn't know how long she had been out for, but she woke suddenly when East, who's shoulder she was resting on, began yelling out in his sleep.

"Run! Run! Run!" he shouted. Dori sat straight up and tried to soothe him back to sleep. North sat up as well, watching his friend tormented in the one place North couldn't reach him, his mind.

"East … East. It's Dori, you're having a bad dream. It's okay, you're okay." she tried soothing him.

It took East a few moments before Dori's words woke up him. He looked around, slightly embarrassed, as both of his companions started assessing whether or not he was okay.

"Sorry," was all he said in response, and then he gently pried himself away from Dori, stood up and started stretching. The sun had finally started streaking across the sky, illuminating a little more about their surroundings. North and Dori stood up too, all three taking a moment to assess what they were seeing. It wasn't just the front porch that was covered in garbage. The yard that looked overrun by the forest also held old furniture of all kinds. Piles of forgotten clothing, and an old broken-down wagon.

"Wow. How did we not see all of this a few hours ago?" Dori asked, walking up to the front door area and began looking inside, finding it much in the same shape as the outside. Every surface was covered in something. A collection of items, most of them broken or knocked over.

"It can't be safe to be in there," Dori spoke out loud, and it didn't surprise her when North walked by her defiantly, as if he didn't have time for her negative attitude.

"Doing it anyway. West, bud, it's North! I'm coming in! Also, sorry about your door!" he apologized. East stood behind Dori, ushering her to follow North inside.

North followed the only path he could once he entered the cottage. It was a disaster. How could his friend be living like this? Garbage piled up, everything piled up. There was barely room to move around in the place. And the smell was less than desirable.

Walking around as carefully as he could, North was so busy looking for signs of a struggle, which was hard to separate from the dirt and garbage everywhere, that he almost missed it. Almost. A certain pile of seemingly forgotten clothes just happened to slightly shake as he walked around it.

East and Dori were coming up behind him but North gestured at them to stop in their tracks. He knelt and did his best impression of someone who had all the patience and time in the world.

"West," he said quietly. "It's North. You can come out; we don't want to hurt you." The pile started shaking again. Slowly, North started pulling off pieces of fabric and forgotten clothing. He kept going until he found a mop of tangled, golden hair. Slowly the hair lifted up until two eyes were staring back at them.

"Hey, man. It's just us. You're safe." North whispered.

West's golden eyes clocked Dori immediately as North tried to lure him out of hiding. Dori could see the fear pouring out of him and immediately felt for him. What things had he seen to cause such a visceral reaction? Dori offered up a small smile, trying to look as harmless as possible.

"Oh her? She's a friend. She won't hurt you." The softness in North's voice surprised Dori. Then again, all he did was bark orders at her and constantly question everything about her.

Seeing that West was taking a good look at her, Dori did her best to put on her most innocent, peaceful face. It was clear this man had been through some things. For a grown ass man to be hiding in a pile of clothes, shaking the way he was, he had some experiences that clearly none of them expected.

"I brought East with me. Can you see him? We've had a wild time, just wait until we tell you about it. Sorry, we sort of camped out on your porch for a few hours, but we didn't know you were in here." North continued explaining. West looked at East and gave him a slight smile, and then looked back at North.

"Are ... are they ... gone?" he asked, his voice sounding cracked and frail.

"No one is here but us. Did the Enchantress send someone to talk to you?" North questioned him, knowing instantly what had happened when West nodded. This all happened because of them. His friend was attacked because of them.

"They banged on my door, and when I wouldn't answer it, they broke my door." West responded.

Dori's heart broke at the way he sounded. A grown man was sitting in front of them, and yet the fear coming off him made him sound like a lost little child hiding from the monster under his bed.

East stepped forward and knelt beside North. He held his hand out to his friend as a sign of comfort and support.

"That's my fault. They aren't happy with me. But I promise you, no one is here right now. Please come out." East explained.

It warmed Dori from the inside out to see these two giants, these two rough men, curl themselves up trying to keep their ferocity away from their terrified friend.

West slowly started unwrapping himself from the safety net he was in and, using East's hand to balance, he stood up. Even the clothes on his back looked like they had seen better days. East and North stood slowly with him and East just held his arms out. West hesitated for a moment, looking around. After deciding that it was, indeed, safe, he launched himself into East's arms.

"It was awful! They were so loud, and they were going to hurt me!" West started to sob. East did his best to rub his friends back but the look he gave North was anything but sweet. It was a look, a promise, that they would have their revenge on whomever did this to their friend.

"Shhh … it's okay. We're here now, we won't let them do anything to you." East was speaking in low tones, doing his best to keep things calm. Dori stood back, letting the three friends have this moment. All three of them had suffered some type of trauma at the hands of this Enchantress. Dori wasn't sure if she wanted to know all the dirty details, or if it would be too much.

"I'm so happy to see you guys! Thank you for coming for me!" West whimpered.

Watching him sob and feeling the emotions rolling from him was more than she could bear. Dori couldn't stop the tears from streaming down her own face. Once again Dori was asking herself what kind of place treated people like this. The longer she stayed here the more she wanted to go back to her own life. Of course, not until she could find a way to help heal these very obviously broken individuals.

Looking around the cabin from where she was standing, Dori could see evidence that this was once maybe a happy home. Underneath the dirt, the garbage, the grime, Dori could see furniture that had been carefully crafted. There were broken dishes all over but if she looked closely, she could see that there had been hand painted designs on it all. This was someone's home, someone loved the things here, and the Enchantress had allowed her men to come in and smash it like it didn't matter, and that pissed Dori off.

"Who's the girl?" West asked.

Dori looked back at them as all three men were looking at her. East with smiling eyes, North with a face of stone, and West with some curiosity, but also caution. Dori gave them a small wave but let the other two speak for her.

"That's what we need to talk to you about," North stated, pulling West's attention back to him. North took a deep breath before continuing.

"She has the crystal."

West's eyes went wide as he looked back at her. The crystal in her pocket started vibrating once again and felt like it was warming up. What kind of magical land had she fallen into?

Chapter 9

"Not the … actual crystal?" Wests asked, his eyes welling up with more tears that he didn't want to shed. If this woman was indeed carrying the crystal, that could change everything. East crossed his arms and nodded his head while North nodded in agreement.

Dori stepped closer to West and put her hand in her pocket, ready to bring the crystal out to make sure everyone was talking about the same piece of rock.

"Do you want to see it?" Dori offered. She didn't want to take it out in case West had the same reaction that East had when he first saw it. Immediately West started shaking his head back and forth while trying to retreat from her.

"No, no, no, no, no. That's … that should stay with you." West's voice was still weak, but he made himself clear. His reaction told Dori that this crystal had some power to it. The question running around in her head now was, why didn't North react the same way that East and West did to the crystal. He stared at it and then she put it away, but he didn't freak out when she showed it to him. Why was there such a difference between these three men when it came to the crystal?

East walked up and put an arm around West, a sign of solidarity and support.

"He doesn't mean to be rude, it's just a lot. There are things that we remember and things that we don't. But that crystal, and what it symbolizes, has been in our minds every day since we sent it out." East explained to her.

Dori had dozens of questions that she wanted to ask them, so she just started at the top of the list.

"What do you mean, sent it out? It fell from the sky."

North moved so that he was standing on the other side of her.

"It fell from the sky in your world, because it was looking for you. We sent it out for you." he explained.

All three set of eyes were starting at her, either waiting to see if she would freak out, or accept what they were saying, she wasn't sure.

"This is all starting to sound a lot more serious than a rock falling from space." she stated. Dori had to step back and take a few deep breaths. She could suspend belief a bit, here and there. She'd passed out in her house and had woken up in some kind of magic land. Sure, that she could believe. In this magic land there were curses, corrupt royalty, and giant gorilla-like flying soldiers. Harder to believe, but okay, she was going with it. But a small piece of rock flying through time and space and landing in her front yard, sent by three strangers who had never met her before? Now they were starting to push it.

"It was looking for our salvation, and then you showed up years later. I would say that's serious." East answered her, taking a step closer to her. He wanted her to understand just how important it was. Now that his memories weren't quite as fuzzy, he was starting to sound less like a lost little boy and more like a full-grown adult. Dori shook her head at him.

"I'm no one's salvation. I'm just someone who shouldn't have picked up glowing rocks that fell from the sky." Dori mumbled as she took a few more steps away from the group. The room was too hot, everything was starting to spin. It was starting to sound like she didn't show up here, in this mysterious land, by accident.

The rock in question started warming up in her pocket, again. Dori placed her hand in her pocket and grabbed it, not to pull it out, but just for comfort.

"What are you thinking?" East asked as he watched Dori start to pace back and forth, using the crystal as a worry stone as she constantly rubbed her thumb over it. West stepped back, unconsciously putting North between himself and Dori.

"Confused. I'm thinking that I'm confused." Dori stated, understanding that her actions were starting to look a bit erratic, but this news was a lot to digest.

"Let's hear it. Maybe we can clear a few things up." North spoke up.

North, with his gruff voice, had a way of settling her mind. Given that he was the one shooting at them not that long ago, it was a strange mixture of feelings.

"Okay. So, let's walk through this, just so that I'm on the same page here. Months ago, this land and its people were cursed by an Enchantress. That curse affected the three of you, all in different ways. Some of you have memories of some things and their meanings, but not everything. None of you can remember your real names, I'm assuming because names have power and you not being able to remember yours helps keep you weak. Convenient for the Enchantress, who has done everything that she can to make it so that you can't regain the power you once had to win against her." Dori was out of breath.

"Years, not months ago. It's not just the Enchantress; she has a sister named Briella. And there are four of us, not just three," East chipped in some information. Dori stared at him for a minute, and then continued.

"And this rock that I'm holding …" Dori asked as her hand went to the crystal as a form of comfort once again.

"Emerald." North stated, being the one that corrected her that time. Dori sighed, and then proceeded on.

"Right, emerald. You guys somehow filled it with magic and sent it out into the universe as a last hope. Its job was to find your saviour and bring them back here to help free the land from the curse." The words coming out of her mouth were sounding crazier by the minute.

"Yes," All three men spoke at the same time.

"No," Dori countered with her own response.

"No?" West piped up on his own that time, and instantly it made Dori feel guilty for taking away his hope. But she wasn't who they thought she was.

"No, I'm not anyone's saviour. In fact, two of you have saved me multiple times since I've been here." It was important to her that all three of them understood that she wasn't here to take charge in anyway. She wanted to help, of course, but they couldn't be putting all their hopes on her. They would only end up disappointed in the end. East took a small step forward.

"There are a few details missing in your assessment. It's not a curse, it's multiple curses. I'm fairly sure each of us had a curse placed on us. The memories are choppy, but from what I can piece together, we were working our own spell, as a last-ditch effort. The last thing we did as free fae was funnel our magic into that emerald, hoping it would give it enough juice to find you and transport you here. And can I just say, looks like it fucking worked." East explained.

North and West nodded in agreement, but Dori still wasn't convinced.

"How are you even remembering any of this? East, it was only yesterday that you couldn't even remember your friends, and now suddenly the history of your land is right at your fingertips?" Dori asked. She didn't want to sound judgemental, but the information was flowing out of him far too quickly.

"It's hard to describe. I don't know if it's being around you and the crystal, or being close again with North and now West, but it's like fragments of my past are slowly being knitted together." East said, looking a bit confused still.

"I have a theory that the reason they kept us apart all of these years was to prevent this very thing from happening. If we were allowed to live in the same place, maybe it would have worn down parts of the curse." North added.

"Why would you just being around each other have any effect on the curse?" Dori asked, her head spinning.

"Simply put, magic. Good magic works best when intentions are pure. We're family. Maybe not technically, but we chose to be family. We've trained together, bled together, celebrated and mourned together. We bonded our life forces together decades ago. That thread that ties us all together can only fully be severed in death. The Enchantress must know that. Keeping us apart was the only way to ensure we had no chance of breaking the curses. Now, of course, with you here, with that emerald here, and with the three of us together, our life forces are trying to heal us." North sounded confident when he talked, but Dori still had questions.

"If it's your magic in here, why won't any of you touch it?" Dori tapped her pocket instead of bringing the crystal out.

"Our magic is tied to our identities. If we, in any way, touch that stone before we remember who we are the magic inside won't recognize us and might lash out." It made sense, everything that they were saying. And yet, Dori just kept shaking her head. Calling someone a saviour put a lot of pressure on her.

"I'm just a girl from a farm. I'm not anyone's saviour." The more she said it, the more it sounded like she wasn't trying to convince them, but instead she was trying to convince herself.

North stepped up to her, not giving her anymore space to back up or to look away from him.

"Now, I've only known you a short while, and I can already tell you that you are more than meets the eye." he stated. At this point East and West had each taken a step back, giving North and Dori space to work out what this all meant.

"What do you expect me to do? March into, what, a castle? What then? I don't know how to fight, the best I can do is knock them over the head with a bucket of water! I'm not meant for fighting! I'm not a warrior." Dori told him sternly. There was something about arguing with North that had Dori's hackles up. He kept stating things like they were facts, but he never asked her for her opinion on the subject.

"Do all the people of your world have such a lack of confidence in themselves? The stone and the magic inside of it travelled through realms to find you. It did *not* make a mistake." North fiercely told her. While he wasn't getting louder, the softness he had while speaking to West was gone. Instead, his voice was firm and confident.

"And if I don't want to?" Dori squeaked out, trying not to panic.

"Then our lands and our people are doomed for eternity to be spelled by the Enchantress. South will never take the throne back, and everything will remain in ruins, forever." North explained bluntly. Dori took a moment to process what he just said. The weight of what would happen if she just walked away was almost enough to knock her over.

"Wait, South? Who is he and why is he supposed to be King?" she asked. Everything was moving so fast, and they were throwing more information at her than she could digest.

"That's another thing. There are four of us, and we're what you would call fae royalty. This land that you're in? It's our kingdom. East, West, and myself, we're the guardians. It's our job to work with South to make sure that balance is achieved. To make sure that everyone stays safe and to protect the kingdom and its people against those who would want to hurt them. He's our rightful King, but the Enchantress took over that position when she cursed Oz." North responded, waiting for her to fully process what he was saying. Dori, to her credit, didn't immediately faint. But the room did start spinning.

"Okay, now I have to sit down. I need fresh air." Dori hurried out the front door and then crouched down and sat on the cold, wooden deck, putting her head between her legs. She heard the scuffing of boots and then felt a body sit down beside her. To her surprise, when she looked up West was sitting there. Not making eye contact, but instead picking at the rocks and dirt in front of him.

"It's scary. I know, more than most, how scary it can be. I spent who knows how long hiding in my cabin, jumping at every sound. Its exhausting being that scared of everything. I don't quite remember the things North does, but I do know this. No one is going to stop them. I'm not the only one who goes to bed every night afraid, because of them." West mumbled.

Dori could feel a lump start to grow in her throat. Every word West spoke was filled with concern and fear.

"I know it's scary, but you really are our best chance. The three of us, well four with South, we wish more than anything we could take away the suffering that our people are going through. But we can't." West started to get choked up.

Dori had to stop him there.

"I can't either." She told him.

West finally looked up and into Dori's eyes.

"Are you sure? The emerald thinks you can. North thinks you can. East certainly thinks you can. And you know what? I think you can, too." he responded.

Dori could feel her defenses starting to waver. It wasn't fair of them to put the most tormented and traumatized person in front of her, she would never turn someone like that down.

"And if I fail?" Dori asked.

West shrugged his shoulders.

"Then you fail. But at least you will have tried. My people are suffering, Dori. I'd give every last scrap of my life force for them, if I could." he told her. The conviction in his speech touched a place in Dori's heart. From where she was sitting, he had already given so much. All three of them had.

"Where would we even begin?" Dori asked him, looking over at North, who had made his way outside, knowing he would be the one with a plan.

"Well." North stepped closer to them. "First things first, we should try breaking these curses surrounding us. If we can do that, we might stand a chance, marching on the castle." he theorized. East walked up, nodding in agreement.

"Where do we even begin figuring out how to do that?" Dori asked. Not knowing anything about the land was really starting to be a deficit. Dori like being the one that figured things out, and in this land, she had to rely on the knowledge of others. It wasn't something she was used to doing.

"I know someone. Someone I haven't visited since the curse started. She lives in the forest on the other side of town." North stated.

Dori took one last look at West, who was staring at her with an innocent wonderment. Dori slowly stood up, dusting off her pants as she rose. West followed suit, standing in front of her.

"Well, looks like we have a lead. Let's go talk to this forest person. Let's go free your people." Dori replied, giving West a slight smile and was surprised when he threw his body into a hug with her. He almost seemed surprised himself. Pulling back, he brushed his hair away from his eyes.

"Thank you, Dori." He graciously thanked her.

With that the four of them took off once more down the road.

Chapter 10

The sun was rising over the horizon as they were walking down the road, and the day was heating up. Dori took off her extra layer and handed it back to East, who was talking quietly with West.

Giving them their privacy, Dori stepped back and in line with North. Watching West and East talking with each other, Dori could see the bond that they shared, and she couldn't imagine how it felt being kept away from the people that meant the most to her. Glancing at North, Dori asked, "So, who's South?"

North glanced over at her and then back at the men in front of them, but he didn't answer her. After another moment of silence Dori tried again.

"How did you all meet? Did you grow up together?" Dori hoped North would give her an answer. The road was long, and a little conversation would make the time go quicker. Dori was full of questions about what was happening and now seemed like the perfect opportunity to get some answers. Just when she thought North wasn't going to speak, he proved her wrong.

"South was, or is, one of us. The four of us grew up together, training for the roles we were going to fill as adults." North answered, pausing to pull out a waterskin and take a sip before continuing on.

"We always knew that we would become the guardians of this land. The ones to protect it, to keep everything in balance. We trained in combat, in a variety of magics, and in battle tactics. But everything we learned, we learned together as a group." North went on explaining.

West and East still talked back and forth in front of them, arms moving around as they updated each other on what had happened for the past ten years.

"Individually we each have our own strengths, of course, but together as a unit we're stronger in every way." North sighed as he replied, feeling the weight of being separated from his friends, his family for ten years.

"How did she separate you? The Enchantress, I mean." Dori asked, hanging on his every word. She could feel the pain in his voice, but she could also feel the love he had for his friends.

"She's a sneaky little bitch, that's how." He spat his answer out in anger. "This feeble woman showed up at the castle one day, in rags, wounds all over like she had been beaten. We had an open-door policy with our people. If something serious was going on we encouraged them to come straight to us so that we could handle it before it could harm anyone else. So, when this woman in torn up rags showed up, we asked her inside. We gave her food and water, and the four of us sat down and listened to her story. We were fools."

North was clenching and unclenching his fists, trying to keep the rage to a minimum as he told his story.

"She told us that, while she was traveling down the road to town, she was jumped by a couple of bandits. They beat her and took all of her belongings before running off. She had the wounds to prove it, so we believed her. We let her stay in the castle while we searched high and low for the bandits, but nothing ever came of the search. Since she wasn't from around here, we told her we would give her lodging until we could find her a more permanent place to stay. She took advantage of our hospitality and within a couple of days she had everything she needed from us to curse us."

East and West became quiet up ahead and listened to North's story to Dori.

"One night, during supper, we all started feeling a bit strange. We started feeling weak and our magic started draining from us. She had poisoned our food without us knowing. It was then that she revealed her true self. She had placed a glimmer on herself, to appear feeble and poorly. When she took it off, we saw her for what she was, a powerful Enchantress, however by then it was too late for us to do anything. We tried fighting back, and for a moment it looked like we had a shot. It was four against one. What we didn't know was that she had snuck her apprentice, her younger sister Briella, into the castle. In our weakened state we were no match for the two of them. The last thing we could think of was to use the little magic we had left to send out a distress signal. The three of us barely had time to pull it off before she found us and placed the final curse on us."

Dori was quiet as North explained their downfall to her. She didn't know what to say, what would bring him comfort. She was curious about one thing, though.

"North, what happened to South? Why wasn't he with you?"

West and East both stopped walking and turned to North and Dori. The four of them stood in the middle of the road.

"South was the most compromised. He was the most powerful of us all. He had the perfect combination of everything. His magic was powerful, his battle tactics were superior, and even his compassion and empathy outshone each of ours. He was our King. The Enchantress dosed his food twice as much as ours. When it was obvious that we were about to lose the fight, he told us to run while he distracted the Enchantress and Briella. He was the only reason we all made it out of that room to call for help. In the end, they kept him hostage. From what I can tell they are keeping him in that room, still keeping him under their power. It's easier to control him that way. The people still see someone they recognize on the throne, but it's been painted as a marriage. He sits on the throne, but the Enchantress controls it, and him, and everything that happens throughout the lands. Briella helped the Enchantress build up a defense of those horrible creatures with their magic to act as their personal guard. Everyone else in the army are either spelled to do as they're told, or their too scared to fight back." North finished his story, looking distraught at having to bring up those memories.

Dori felt almost woozy after hearing their story. North took a deep breath, and then walked around the rest of the group.

"So, who is South? He's the best one out of all of us. And they took him from us." With that North was done talking and started back down the road.

West turned and caught up with North, placing an arm on North's shoulder for a minute before letting it drop and walking in silence beside him. East turned to Dori and gestured for her to start walking with him.

"He blames himself, of course. North always did take on far more responsibility than was asked of him. Not one of us knew she was lying, not one of us knew what she was up to. But North, he doesn't blame us as a group. He blames himself." East explained.

"That has to be a terrible feeling." Dori stated, finding it hard to imagine taking all of that on, and then being forced to live alone with nothing to distract her from those thoughts.

"It is. I wish, more than anything, that I could take all that from him. That weight that he carries won't let up until the four of us are reunited and that bitch and her sister are put in the ground. Even then, I don't know that he'll ever fully forgive himself." East said with concern in his voice for his friend.

Dori took another look at North. His exterior was crafted to keep people away. He was gruff and rude. There was nothing about him that was inviting. Only now, Dori could see it for the façade that it was. Keeping people away meant he couldn't get anyone else hurt.

"How are you feeling, by the way? Your memories seem to be coming back."

East smiled at her.

"They are and they aren't. Small things are coming back, slowly. Listening to West and North talk about their experiences has helped. It's murky, like I'm trying to look through muddy water to see the bottom of the lake. I know it's there, and if I try hard enough maybe I catch a glimpse. There is still so much I don't remember." East shrugged, the lack of memory was something he had gotten used to. Memories taking time to resurface didn't phase him much, mostly because he never thought the day would come where they came back. Looking at the fields that they were walking past, with the blue skies and birds chirping, Dori wouldn't have known how broken this world was if it wasn't for these men.

Dori walked quietly beside East for a few moments and took notice of the changing landscape. When they were outside of West's cabin they were surrounded by old forests and bush. It had slowly changed, and they were back to the fields filled with crops and circling birds.

In the distance shapes started forming as they walked closer to town. Every step closer brought those buildings more and more into view, and for Dori every step closer to civilization had her heart beating faster.

Dori wasn't sure what to expect, would the Enchantress's guards be out hunting for them? Would the town be overrun with nowhere to hide? North had explained that the fastest way to get to where they were going was to go through the city and not around it. Going around would at least add two days travel, and since Dori was sure they were all wanted fugitives, the longer they were out in the open and vulnerable the most likely it was that the wrong someone would see them.

Walking into the city, however, came with its own risks. It would be close to midday, so the streets shouldn't be so empty. Being able to blend into a crowd would be their best shot, Dori hoped it all went according to plan so that they could get in and out before the Enchantress and Briella even knew they were there.

As it turned out, no one was prepared for what they walked into. There were no people to be found. East, West, and North all looked visibly shocked as they started making their way through the streets. There were no civilians and no guards down any street or in any building. The city looked abandoned.

Chapter 11

Every street they turned down broke Dori's heart. There was no laughter here. There was no life here. The city wasn't just abandoned, it looked as if a bomb had gone off. The crunch of rock underneath their feet echoed through the empty streets. Buildings had windows broken out of them and doors kicked in. It all looked the way West's cabin had looked.

Personal items littered the streets, appearing as if they were stomped on and destroyed. Children's toys, broken dishes, ripped clothing. The more she saw, the more Dori concluded that these people were terrorized, forced from their homes for unknown reasons. Dori sent up a silent prayer, asking for no bodies to be found amongst the rubble. Her hope was that everyone who wanted out got out.

"Keep an eye out. Even though it looks empty, the Enchantress has spies everywhere." North's gruff voice filled Dori with a small bit of comfort. East and West unconsciously flanked Dori while North took the lead. All four of them kept constantly scanning for threats as they kept their conversations to a minimum.

It wasn't until they were closer to the middle of the city that signs of life started to appear, but it wasn't what they thought they would find. It wasn't innocent citizens going about their day to day lives. It was more of what East and Dori had encountered. The elite were still around, seemingly oblivious to the devastation that surrounded their city. It appeared that they still walked around with their greasy hairstyles and their high fashion clothes.

Making sure to stick to the shadows and walk in twos, East with Dori and North with West, no one uttered a word. They made sure to move out of the way of anyone walking towards them and doing their best not to make eye contact with anyone.

Down the road a few small businesses started to appear, but the dead look in the eye of the employees didn't sit right with Dori. Their faces were pale and blank, and their movements were very calculated. There was no chatter, and no one smiled. Either they were being forced to stay or they had no way out.

It dawned on Dori that not everyone would be able to just pack up and leave. Some had family members that wouldn't be able to travel. Others wouldn't be able to feed their families at all if it wasn't for the measly sums they were earning by working for the higher up citizens.

Before they were discovered, North ushered Dori down a side street. Her stomach twisted at the contrast of the overly gluttonous elite being served by the broken down under class.

There was a lot that needed to be fixed here. Looking even closer at the broken-down homes, Dori could see what she had missed before. Though the buildings looked condemned, in some of them there were tiny signs of life. Not everyone had gotten out.

"They must be hiding somewhere. But where would the Enchantress's guards not be able to see them?" West finally spoke up, asking the questions all of them were thinking. North was the only one with an answer.

"I have a hunch. Deep in the forests there is a magic that is not controlled by any one person. It has been known to protect and shield those looking for refuge." he explained.

While it sounded strange to Dori, a forest using magic to protect its people was on par for things that made sense in this land.

"Hasn't it also been known to have its own guardian keeping an eye on things?" East interjected.

"What kind of guardian?" Dori asked, not sure what kind of answer she was hoping for.

"A witch," West whispered, and Dori's eyebrows shot up.

"A witch? Isn't the kingdom in this mess because of a witch?" Dori questioned.

How many of them were running around? East put his hand on her shoulder to steady her.

"Different kind of witch. The one in the forest, she's a good witch. Pure of heart, glowing with kindness, you know the type," North grunted. Dori, however, did not know the type. Everything was brand new information to her, a fact that North kept forgetting. East continued North's thought, seeing the confusion on Dori's face.

"The people look to her in times of trouble when the four of us are otherwise occupied. When we're out securing the borders, people know that they can go to her in the forest, and they will be protected until we get back. I don't know how much the people have been told about our absence, but I'm sure those that could, flocked to her did when things started going downhill around here." North kept glancing around the corners of the alley to make sure they weren't gaining any attention.

"Well, if she's a witch, why doesn't she go fight off the ones who are holding the land in such a chokehold?" Dori asked. This time West was the one to answer her, albeit in a quiet whisper.

"It's not that simple. You've got multiple witches against one. You've got evil versus good." he explained.

"Not to mention that most of the energy and power she had would be going towards keeping these people safe. Magic, at least good magic, doesn't come from an endless well of power. There are limits to it. If it came down to keeping people safe and hidden versus fighting two witches and maybe losing, I know what she would be choosing." East walked over to North and to help him keep an eye out.

"I gather that's where we're headed to." North looked back and nodded to Dori, confirming her thoughts.

"She may also have some idea on how to get out from under the thumb of these curses. Until we break them, we have no hope in defeating the sisters, getting our King back, or freeing our people." North gestured for West and Dori to follow him back out of the alley.

"Alright, let's get out of here. We've lucked out up until now, but I won't feel safe until we are out of the city limits." North explained. The four of them exited the alley and walked right into a small mob of munchkies. There had to be at least twelve of them. There was one in the middle, holding a piece of pipe like a sword. Dori's heart jumped into her throat as West slipped behind North for protection.

"Looks like we found some more garbage in our town," the munchkie proclaimed. The group behind him followed it up with loud shouts filled with anger.

Dori's hands started to shake at the sight of the angry mob. East subtly moved towards her, angling his body to be just in front of her. North straightened up, puffing his chest out slightly, at the same time adjusting his body to completely center himself in front of his friends. Looking at the munchkie who appeared to be the leader, North spoke.

"You don't want to do this. Walk away, while you can."

That caused the mob to burst out laughing, their leader taking two steps towards North, showing him that they held no fear.

"You might have been something to fear a long time ago, but now you are powerless." The munchkie spat at North's feet, sneering and adjusting his grip on the metal pipe. West started to shake behind North and his eyes were shut in fear. Dori adjusted her stance to be closer to him, putting her hand on the back of his arm, hoping it would provide him with a bit of relief. He wasn't in this alone, his friends were with him and would protect him.

North looked down at his feet and then back up.

"What makes you think I need my magic to be someone you should fear?"

The munchkie stepped forward again.

"Without that magic, you have no ..."

North struck first, plowing his fist straight into the munchkie's nose so hard that Dori heard the crunching of bone. The munchkie's head snapped back as he screamed out in pain. North then quickly grabbed the pipe out of his hands and swung it at the munchkie's knees, smashing the bone there as well. It all happened so fast; the rest of the mob was in shock.

Dori stood there, almost in awe at how fast North took control of the situation without backing down. If he was this fierce without magic, she could only imagine how deadly he was when he had his full power. North lifted the pipe up onto his shoulders and looked up at the rest of the mob with a look of rage on his face.

"Anyone else?" was all he had to say before chaos broke loose. The mob started yelling and running towards them. Seeing that most of the mob was heading towards North, Dori pulled West out of the way, putting him behind her.

East came alive, throwing himself into the mob and striking out wherever he could. Every punch he threw knocked someone to the ground. Some of them stayed down, while others took a moment and then got back up and jumped back into the brawl.

North was busy pulling munchkies to himself and then headbutting them, knocking them down. After blood started dripping down his forehead, he pushed back and just started swinging the pipe at anyone that dared get close to him. The two fighters were in their element, working together as if in a dance. Both keeping an eye on the how the crowd was moving and both of them cutting off anyone who appeared to be trying to get behind them to West and Dori.

Dori saw it before North did. One of the munchkies he dropped with a headbutt pulled out a dagger from under the back of his shirt, and he lunged towards North with it, intent on stabbing him in the side.

"North! Behind you!" Dori shouted out, hoping he could hear her above all the yelling. Whether or not he did, he turned just in time to redirect the arm with the dagger, grabbing the arm it was attached to, and using his elbow to break the forearm on the munchkie. He then grabbed the falling dagger, flipped it around, and flung it at a stray munchkie who heard Dori and started running towards her. The dagger hit right at the base of the spine, embedding itself completely and dropping the munchkie, who could no longer feel his legs.

Without skipping a beat North turned back into the mob and kept going. East's face and shirt were full of blood spatters by the end of the brawl, where he dropped the last guy before looking over at North.

"I've missed this. Though, you're getting soft. I definitely dropped more munchkies than you this time." The smirk on

Easts face told Dori just how much he enjoyed getting his hands dirty. North raised an eyebrow at him.

"They must have scrambled your brains even more than I thought, if you think you dropped more than me. Delusional." North walked over to East as they gave each other a small fist bump on the shoulder. As if they both shared a thought in that moment, they started looking around in a panic. Dori knew what they were looking for, or in this case, who.

"He's right here. He's safe," Dori stated as she shifted slightly so that they could see West curled up behind her, with his hands gripping the back of her shirt so hard his knuckles were turning white.

"Is it over?" West asked, with his eyes tightly shut. Any victorious feelings that they were sharing dulled as they saw the fear rolling off their friend. Both men walked over to West, stepping over the bodies on the ground. Each man took one of Wests hands and started unclenching them from Dori's shirt.

"It's over. You're safe, West." East waited until both hands were free before he pulled West into a hug. West clung to him and let out the sob that he was holding in. Trauma didn't always resolve itself quickly. Dori felt how hard West was shaking during the fight. He would be fighting off the effects of the curse for a long time. It was very possible that he would never fully feel safe again.

Feeling a tap on her shoulder, Dori looked up at North, who had heartbreak written all over his face, heartbreak for his friend.

"Thank you. For him." Four words. Four words that she wasn't expecting to hear. Four words that she didn't need to hear, she would have done it no matter what. But four words that she knew weren't easy for him to say, and yet he did. For his friends. The enigma that was North was becoming her favorite kind of puzzle.

"Of course." North nodded at her, and she nodded back, lost in his eyes. They were saying so much without saying anything at all. The wall he held himself behind was starting to thaw around her and she was catching glimpses of the man East boasted about. The man West looked up to. The moment was gone a second later as East and West separated, and North stepped back.

"Unless we want to do that again, we should be running. Now." With that North turned and started walking away. East slung an arm around West's waist, using his other hand to hold onto West's hand, helping him down the street. West was trying to hold in his sobs as he was escorted past Dori. For a brief moment he made eye contact with her and mouthed the words 'thank you'. Dori dipped her head in acknowledgement, and then turned and followed behind the three of them as they started hurrying out of the city.

Chapter 12

While they were speeding through the city limits, North swung around and ended up beside Dori. He held his hand out to her and when she looked down, she saw the munchkie's dagger in it, handle facing towards her. Dori looked up at him, confusion flittering across her face.

"Take it. In case we find ourselves in a similar situation." Dori looked back down on it and hesitated.

"It won't bite, just take it." North shoved it towards her even more and that time, on instinct, she grabbed the handle. North pulled his hand back before she could return it to him.

"If that happens again and one of the munchkies manages to make it past me and East, I want you to pull that out and stab anyone who gets within five feet of West. You also use it even if you aren't guarding West. I don't want any munchkie to get within five feet of you either, so you use that if, and when you need it. You'll probably only get one good shot in, so make it count."

Dori started examining the dagger as they walked.

"What happens if I can't take someone down with one shot? What if I stab them and they keep coming?" The words coming out of her mouth sounded so foreign to her. Never in her life had she been a fighter, and here she was, talking about stabbing someone for getting too close to her.

"You call me. You say my name, and I will find my way to you." The seriousness in his voice took Dori by surprise.

"What if you don't hear me?" Until a few moments ago, Dori never realized how loud a brawl could get. Everyone was yelling, bones were breaking followed by screams. North grabbed her arm, stopping her so she would look up at him.

"Say my name. Call for me. I'll hear you, and I'll come for you." he stated confidently.

Dori was glad he had stopped her, or she would have tripped over her feet at that last statement.

"Even if we're across the brawl from each other?" Dori whispered, unable to breathe properly at the intensity coming from North's eyes.

"Even if I have to behead every motherfucker that dares to stand between us. You're one of us, now. You're family. And I fucking protect my family." Unable to look away from each other, Dori and North stood there, staring into each other's eyes. A high pitch whistle pulled North's eyes from her, allowing her to look down and away.

East had made it to the edge of the city with West, and they were looking back for North and Dori. Without uttering a word North grabbed Dori's empty hand and led her to the others. When they reached East, North dropped her hand and started walking ahead once again. East eyed up the dagger in Dori's other hand.

"Maybe tuck that away. Just to be on the safe side." Dori nodded, tucking it in the back of her pants and pulling her shirt over top to cover it. As they started walking again Dori took a moment to take a deep breath. She wasn't sure what was happening here, but the more she was around North the harder it was to breathe properly.

As they exited the city limits it became almost unnaturally quiet. The road they were taking started to lead back down into the forest. The trees themselves were almost standing unnaturally still. There were no bugs or bird sounds, nothing but their feet on the brick. North and East shared a quick glance with one another before ushering West and Dori to stand in the middle of the road, while North and East each flanked the outside.

Dori's nerves were shot. She wasn't ready for another brawl this soon, even though she was more armed than before. West looked like he was just getting a handle on his emotions, another brawl now would break him. A random branch cracking in the distance had all four of them on alert. For a moment Dori thought she heard something crawling around in the trees. A shadow passed from one tree to another, but it was gone so fast she wasn't sure what she saw. The forest was becoming denser, the shadows growing as the sunlight couldn't fully penetrate the canopy.

Without any prior thought, Dori reached out for West's hand, which he gladly gave her. There was no judgement in her action, no resentment at having to reassure a full-grown warrior. All Dori wanted to do was make sure he knew he wasn't alone, and that it was alright to be scared.

Suddenly there was a rustling in the bushes ahead, before two groups of five, one on each side of the road, walked out of the forest and onto the road, blocking their way forward. It wasn't munchkies, much to Dori's relief. These were citizens of the land. They looked a little worn around the edges, dirt marking their clothes, tired circles around their eyes. They were holding wooden staffs and small daggers in their hands. A few of them had fashioned camouflage by using the leaves of the trees in their hair.

For a few moments no one moved, no one said a word. Both groups assessing each other, looking for threats.

East was the first to break the silence.

"We mean no harm; we're just passing through."

"Turn around. No one is welcome past this road. You're trespassing," one of the men in the middle of the group spoke up.

"Trespassing? This is a public road. Move." North was a little less polite than East, but they had been through a lot and his patience had run out.

"Not a public road anymore. Turn around before we make you turn around."

West tensed beside Dori while North and East stood a little straighter.

"You could try, but you wouldn't like the results. Now move." North barely tried to keep the annoyance out of his voice.

"What business do you have down that road?" A woman stepped around the spokesman and addressed North.

"Visiting a friend." The tension was only building as neither group was willing to yield their place on the road.

"How do we know you're not hunting someone down for the Enchantress? You may be Guardians, or at least you used to be. But now one of you sits on the throne, side by side with a vile and cruel Enchantress. How do we know that you don't service her the same way?" the spokesman spat. North growled back at him before East answered.

"South doesn't want to be there, I assure you. Not all can be explained right now, however know that our intentions are good and true. Besides, what do we look like to you, a group of munchkies?"

Dori saw a few members of the group looking at North and East in confusion, as if they were puzzles to be figured out.

"Tell us who you're looking for. If we know them, we'll escort you." It sounded like a trick to Dori, but North must have seen something she didn't.

"The witch of the woods. Goes by the name Elowynn." At the mention of her name the forest started to come back to life. Bird songs could be heard echoing through the trees.

"What business do you have with her?" another member of the opposing group asked.

"Our business is for us to know." East stated.

Just as the man was about to counter again, a warm wind came out of nowhere and gently circled both groups. A faint voice danced upon the breeze. Dori couldn't quite make out what it was saying, but the group in front of them must have. They slowly parted and gestured to the road behind them.

"She's waiting for you." The main spokesman nodded towards the road before turning and walking down it. It appeared as if they were going to get a personal escort to the witch of the woods.

North made sure he was the one leading the group, with Dori and West directly behind him, East behind them all, watching their backs. Both groups walked in silence, keeping an eye on each other.

The road seemingly came to a dead end, but their escort turned into the forest and when it was Dori's turn to follow, she spotted a hidden path. As they moved through the forest, Dori could sense others around them that they couldn't yet see. Whether they were hiding in the trees or using magic to veil their presence, Dori understood just how outnumbered they were. Through the trees and bushes they were led, until they came to the opening of a small cave. That's where their escorts stopped.

"Where is she?" East asked, politely. Before anyone could answer, Dori spotted someone walking out of the cave.

Out from the darkness of the cave came a woman with small purple flowers and dark green ivy wound through her golden-brown hair. Atop her head sat a crown made of branches and twigs. Her arms were wrapped with vines, her eyes as green as a fern, and her skin dusted with dirt. The dress she wore was a moss green with what appeared to be wildflowers growing up the side of it. One of the more shocking discoveries for Dori was that this woman was completely bare foot. Her toes looked to be stained with dirt up to her ankles. Dori leaned over to North to whisper.

"Who is that?" It took North a moment to answer her back.

"Dori, meet Elowynn. The forest witch."

Elowynn gave the group a small smile, dimples appearing on either side of her mouth. A small bird flew to Elowynn, landing on the palm of her hand for a brief moment. Elowynn smiled at the bird, used a very gentle touch to pet the top of its head, and then lifted her hand, shooing the bird off into the bushes once more.

Her voice sounded as light as a fairy and her eyes sparkled as she spoke.

"Welcome to the forest of the free, Dori."

Chapter 13

"Please, follow me," Elowynn stated, turning and slowly walking back into the cave. North put his hand on Dori's back, leading her into the cave, with East and West following close behind them.

The inside perimeter of the cave floor was covered with candles, giving off a gentle glow to the space. A variety of rebel citizens were lounging around, all eyes watching Dori, North, East and West as they entered. Elowynn seemed to pay no attention to the tension that filled the room as she wandered over to a small, stone alter on the far wall.

"The spirits told me to expect visitors, but they didn't say it would be the cursed guardians, and they definitely didn't say that the guardians would be bringing a woman from a different world with them."

Dori looked at Elowynn, startled. Was it that obvious that she wasn't from their world?

"Don't worry. You aren't in danger. Well, not in here at least." Elowynn turned slightly taking a good look at Dori, before she turned back to her alter. North was the first one to respond to her.

"We've come to you–"

"I know why you're here, North. You've come to find answers. No longer will you sit idly by while my sisters rule the kingdom you were meant to protect."

Dori almost fell over. The Enchantress, Briella, and Elowynn were sisters? That seemed like an important fact that she maybe should have been told, and yet was kept from her.

"Yes." North looked down at Dori, concern written on his face at her body swaying slightly. Dori gave him a hesitant small smile to show him she was alright. Over the last few days there was a lot of information thrown at her that she didn't know because she didn't grow up in this land. It was exhausting to constantly be learning something that everyone around her already knew.

"The good news is that every curse that my sisters have put upon you, your friends, your people, and this kingdom can be undone, with minimal damage."

Dori stood very still, waiting for the other shoe to drop. North had the same instincts and refused to take his eyes off Elowynn. East took a step forward.

"Okay, what do we need to do? Not to speak for the others, but I'd really like to be back to my old self, with my old memories and strengths, as soon as possible."

Dori looked at him, giving him a friendly smile. Surprisingly West was the next to step forward.

"I would like to stop being afraid of everything, including my own shadow. It's really an exhausting way to live."

Elowynn walked over to him, bringing her hand up to gently caress West's cheek. It wasn't out of pity but understanding.

"That's the part that may be tricky. Each of you has a separate curse that has been put upon you. East, you are under a curse of the mind. North, you are under a curse of the heart. West, a curse of courageousness." Elowynn's voice was broadcasting calmness throughout the cave. The earlier tension was melting away as she talked, and Dori found her worries lifting the longer Elowynn spoke.

"I believe your friend, South, has his own unique curse as well. His is the strongest, a curse of free will. The longer he's under their power the more his magic is being supressed. It won't be easy to break him out of it. And until South's curse is broken, the land and its people will remain affected," Elowynn explained.

"Do you know how to break the curses? If we free East, West, and North, maybe they'll have enough power to break South out." If the curses were all broken, maybe she would be able to find a way home. Dori would never say it out loud, but she thought about it often enough.

Being in this strange land was exciting and dangerous, the adventure of a lifetime. But she couldn't stay here forever. She had to go back to where she belonged at some point. It wasn't worth bringing up to the group now, but Dori had to believe that there was at least hope that she could go back.

"It's possible that, if three of the four guardians were back to full power, they could overpower the Enchantress and Briella, and free the kingdom." Elowynn confirmed.

"Great, what are we waiting for then? Break our curses so we can save our friend." North had little tact in situations like this. Dori nudged him for his lack of patience.

"What you need to understand, North, is that I'm not the one with the power to break the curses. Each curse will need its own unique cure. More than that, a curse is a very powerful spell. To cast more than one curse and have them be as successful as they have been, she would have had to embrace very dark magic. What you need to counter that is someone of pure light and love. Someone full of kindness and hope to be your anchor. Someone who wasn't around when the curses were cast. Someone who has never been touched by the Enchantresses magic."

Letting the weight of that settle, slowly one by one every person in the cave turned to Dori, who looked utterly surprised. When she really thought about it, it started to make sense. The land and its people had been cursed for a decade without any hope or sign that it was going to change. It wasn't until that crystal found her and brought her here that things started happening.

Dori looked over at East first, seeing the hope that he was almost to scared to believe in. From the start he was protective of her, even if he didn't understand why. North, despite being an ass from the very first moment, seemed to be somehow drawn to her, and over the last few days the walls he kept around himself had started to lower. West, who was afraid of everyone and everything, didn't take long to become more comfortable around her. Even going as far as to take shelter behind her during the brawl, believing that she would keep him safe.

She was brought here, from a different land, for a reason. Being in the right place at the right time, in the right land, was far too much of a coincidence for Dori. She knew in her heart that she had it inside of herself to help these men. The only thing she didn't know was how the hell she was supposed to do it. Dori looked back at Elowynn with a lump in her throat.

"Tell me what to do and I'll do it. Tell me how to free my friends." Dori stated, determined to help.

East rushed at Dori, lifting her up and twirling her around. Tears were filling his eyes. The idea that there was hope, that there was someone willing to fight for them and with them, it was emotional for East. He had spent the last decade with people that only wanted to use him. People that didn't care about his well-being.

Dori was everything the munchkies hated. She was kind and loving. Dori was smart, but she never made anyone feel inferior because of it. The day she walked out of the forest and down that yellow brick road, wearing that ridiculous outfit, was the luckiest day of his life. Elowynn cleared her throat and then gestured at East and Dori.

"Let's start here. The curse of the mind. It's not one that can be cured with anything in the physical realm. The battle is going on inside the brain, that is where the curse needs to be broken."

Elowynn started circling East, as if she could see inside of his mind. She looked away, gesturing to her followers that still stood against the walls, watching everything.

"We can't do this here. We need to go up. It's time I show you where we've been staying."

A mere twenty minutes later, Dori couldn't believe where she was standing. Elowynn and her people led them out of the cave and on a small walk deeper into the forest. Right when Dori was weighing whether or not this was a trap, ladders started falling from the trees. When Dori looked up, she saw a sight that could only be described as adult tree houses. East climbed the ladder first, followed closely behind by West. As Dori was preparing to climb the rope ladder up, she saw Elowynn and her people expertly climbing up the other ladders. Once a ladder was no longer in use it was quickly pulled up and out of the way.

Dori lifted her right foot and put it on the bottom rung and the entire ladder swayed with the added weight. Dori gasped and clung on to the ladder. North reached out and held it still.

"Why do we have to climb into the stupid trees anyways?" Dori muttered, embarrassed that North was there to catch her moment of panic. North dipped his head down slightly, catching her eye contact.

"I'll hold it steady down here. You just focus on taking it one step at a time."

Dori nodded and then looked up again at how high she was expected to climb. She could feel the sweat start to build on the palms of her hands, causing her to hold on tight enough that her knuckles were turning white. North reached out and put his hand on top of hers.

"Just breathe. If you fall, I'll be down here to catch you. Now up you go." The tone of his voice had softened for her and a small part of her started to swoon at the gentleness of the moment. That instantly changed when the ladder started to sway again. Dori nodded to him and one rung at a time she climbed the rope ladder. The higher she got the shakier everything seemed to be, and yet Dori didn't dare look down to see how far she had come. She knew the moment she did it would be game over. She would be frozen, and North would have to climb up to rescue her. That was an embarrassment that she refused to put herself through.

Her thoughts distracted her enough that she didn't realize when she made it to the top until there was no more ladder to grab for. Instead, she saw the edge of a platform and two large bodies waiting for her.

"There you are my friend. Come on up." East smiled at her as he and West each grabbed onto one of her arms, hauling her up and away from the edge. Dori's hands shook as she grabbed East's arms before he could step away. He stepped closer, offering his support while she started deep breathing.

"You're okay. Just think, you don't have to do that again. At least, until we have to go back down." The thought of having to climb over the edge to go down had the blood draining from Dori's face as East chuckled.

"Sorry, I'm supposed to be helping. Maybe don't think about that. Just breathe and, for now, walk on the inside."

Dori nodded, quickly crouching down, needing another moment as she heard North coming up from the ladder. Dori watched as a few men pulled the ladder up after North, and then replaced the railing so that it wasn't a safety hazard.

The first thing North did once he was standing was to look for Dori, glancing over her to make sure there were no injuries. It only lasted a second before he was walking away from her and towards Elowynn, who had been standing off to the side, patiently waiting for her guests.

"Wonderful. Now that you're all here, follow me." With that she turned and led the group away. Dori stood up, still slightly wobbly, and followed West, with East at her back, down the narrow platform that seemed to wrap around the tree. Finally looking up to take in her surroundings Dori saw how vast the community had become, up in the trees. There were at least a dozen platforms joined together by a variety of rope bridges. At what appeared to be the center of the community were three tree house structures. The one that Elowynn was leading them towards had been prepped with candles sitting on the floor, in small ceramic dishes.

"This is where we'll break the mind curse," Elowynn stated as she entered the room. She thoughtfully turned to East. "Are you sure you're ready for this? It won't be a pleasant experience."

East barely let her finish her sentence.

"Yes. I'm ready. Get her out of my head."

Elowynn nodded at his answer and turned to start preparing. A random woman walked up to East and Dori, handing them each a small cup filled with cool water. Dori readily accepted it, feeling parched after the events of the day. North walked by, lightly touching her back as he passed as his way of checking in. He walked over to Elowynn and started helping her prepare.

Chapter 14

Dori stood by the doorway, looking into the room where North and Elowynn were preparing for the ceremony. There were two small cots placed next to each other in the middle of the circular room. East had walked into the room and was already sitting on one, wringing his hands together and biting at his lips. Dori didn't blame him for being nervous, her own hands were starting to shake, and doubt kept flooding her mind.

Everyone in this room, even in this village, needed for this ceremony to work. If it didn't work it would show them that she wasn't who they thought she was, and she couldn't help them at all. Dori desperately wanted to be who they needed, if only to return the kindness they showed her by helping them out.

Scanning the room, trying to take it all in, Dori's eyes caught North's and he gave her an assessing stare. If she failed at helping his close friend would their blossoming friendship fade before it had even fully begun?

Elowynn started walking around the room in her bare feet, burning a small bundle of different grasses and using the smoke to cleanse the room. Every person she walked past was encompassed by a cloud of smoke.

North walked over to Dori and leaned on the wall beside her.

"Are you sure you want to give this a try?" He raised his left eyebrow at her. Dori took a moment to think about it. This wasn't something that she should rush in to. But if she was being honest with herself, she had decided the moment Elowynn told them that she was a part of it.

"Yes. Just anxious to know exactly how to do this."

Elowynn looked over but kept preparing the room.

"Mind walking. Everything East needs to break this curse is inside of his head. Something is stopping him, but we have no way of knowing what it is. That's where you come in." Elowynn gestured at Dori.

"I'm going to go into his head?" There were times Dori didn't even want to be in her own head with all the thoughts flying around. What was she going to encounter in the mind of someone from a completely different world? As if sensing her rising panic, East shot her a small smile.

"I wouldn't want it to be anyone else, friend."

Dori looked over at him and the emotion started getting to her. The trust he had in her, and the complete lack of fear, floored her. He was a beautiful soul, inside and out.

Mind walking sounded like an impossible task, and if it wasn't for the extraordinary things that had taken place up to this point in this land, Dori would have thought they were trying to pull a prank on her.

Over in the corner Elowynn was using a mortar and pestle to grind down wild mushrooms in a small wooden bowl. Dori watched with fascination as Elowynn started adding what looked like a few herbs to the bowl and then she took a steaming pot of water, pouring in enough to fill the bowl to the brim.

The smoking grass was sitting on the table beside the bowl and Elowynn picked the bundle up, blowing the smoke into the bowl.

With careful hands Elowynn picked up the steaming bowl and poured equal amounts of the concoction into two separate small wooden cups. She placed the cups on a small serving tray and looked up at Dori.

"It's time. Dori, once you're in there you'll have a better understanding of what needs to be fixed. Don't be surprised if East needs to go through parts of the journey himself, and don't do anything to put yourself in harm's way. The mind is a fickle thing, and if something happens to you in there, I can't guarantee you'll come back unharmed."

Nodding, but not fully hearing Elowynn, Dori took one last look at North, who was watching her carefully, pushed off the doorframe, and walked to the unoccupied cot beside East.

"You don't have to do this, you know." East looked up at her, questions filling his eyes. Giving her one final moment to back out. Understanding the person he was, Dori knew that if she backed out now, he would hold no ill will towards her. He would completely understand and wouldn't hold it against her at all. His was a soul worth saving.

"I know." It was all Dori could say in the moment, as she sat down on the empty cot and took East's hand into hers. East and Dori kept eye contact as Elowynn brought the cups towards them. North couldn't stay away if he tried, slowly circling the cots with his arms crossed, never taking his eyes off them, like a wolf on the prowl.

Elowynn knelt beside the cots, placing the tray on the ground. One at a time she handed East and Dori a cup to their empty hand, all the while muttering something under her breath.

Moving in sync, Dori and East raised the cups to their lips, draining the contents into their mouths. It tasted earthy and warm, with the spice of a fall breeze. The cup was taken out of their hands.

"How fast does this stuff work?" Dori asked, not taking her eyes off East. But before anyone could answer her the room started spinning and Dori's eyelids started getting heavy. The last thing she felt before falling into unconsciousness was someone grabbing her shoulders and guiding her body down to the bed.

Opening her eyes, it didn't take long for Dori to realize where she was. Sitting up it looked like she was lying down in the dirt right beside an old barn. There were a few bales of hay stacked to the side of the door and a chicken coop a little bit further down. Dori could hear the clucks of the chickens on the inside. The ground felt slightly damp, like the dew from the night before hadn't fully evaporated in the sun just yet. And still, while everything looked right, something didn't feel right. The air smelt wrong somehow. She couldn't smell the fresh air, the grass she was sitting on, or even the chicken shit from the coop. Nothing smelt right.

Dori stood up and started looking around. This was a dream, East's dream. She had to find him to help him get answers, but looking around he was nowhere to be seen. Dori wasn't sure if she wanted to start shouting his name out. She may have been inside of a dream, but that didn't mean that she was safe.

Leaning heavily on her instinct Dori started walking in the only direction that felt right, and it was leading her away from the farmhouse and the yard, closer to a dirt path that seemed to be running parallel from the house. As she started walking down it, she felt a small glimmer of hope in her chest and, trusting that it was leading her the correct way, Dori sped up a bit, anxious to find East.

A few minutes into her walk Dori came across a corn field and stopped in her tracks. Sitting in the middle of the field was East. He was rocking back and forth, and his hands were constantly pulling at his hair. Dori could see that he was distressed about something and didn't even notice as she slowly walked up to him. When she got right behind him, she could hear what he was muttering to himself, over and over.

"Think, think, think. Stupid boy. Think, think, think. What happened? Where is everyone? Think, think, think."

Over and over East kept muttering the same thing while he rocked. Looking him over Dori could see the state of his clothes and it wasn't good. His shirt was ripped in a few spots, and he had dirt marks all over his pants. His arms had scratches and bruises everywhere.

Slowly walking around him, so as to not startle East, Dori took stock of his face. Tears were rolling down his dirty cheeks and his left eye was partially swollen. Hands up so as to not startle him, Dori slowly lowered herself into his eyesight, approaching him like she would a stray dog, with her voice calm and low.

"East? Can you hear me?" Dori ended up sitting in front of him, but it took a moment for his eyes to focus on her, lost in his own delirious thoughts, his mind was a million miles away. To his credit he didn't look startled or scared of her once he focused, he simply took his hands out of his hair and grabbed at her arm. His grip was strong as his voice started to shake.

"Where did they go? Where is everyone? You just need to think!" The wild look in his eyes, and panic in his voice grew stronger with every second that went by.

"Where did who go?" Dori was confused, looking around, expecting to see someone. When Elowynn mentioned something was blocking East from breaking the curse Dori was expecting some kind of shadow monster that needed defeating, or physical wall that would need to be torn down. What she wasn't expecting was to find her friend, sitting on the ground, unravelling completely.

"Think, think, think!" East threw her arm away from him and quickly stood up, starting to pace back and forth. Dori followed, stepping back when his pacing got too close.

"East, who are you looking for? Is it North and West? Because they sent me here to find you." Dori hoped their names would draw his attention and help him remember the outside world. East stopped pacing, turning towards Dori and, ignoring her personal space, stepped as close as he could get. He grabbed at her arms again, as if willing her to have all the answers.

"They sent you? Where are they? Why can't I find them?" He was getting desperate. Remembering what Elowynn said about East having to fulfill some type of quest in order for his memory to come back to him, Dori decided to give him just that.

"They're lost, East. They are waiting for you to come and find them." Keeping eye contact with him was important, but not easy. He took a sharp, deep breath as his face went from panic to concern.

"They are? We have to go find them. They must have been waiting for so long." He grabbed her hand and started pulling her back to the dirt path. His rough hand grasping on to her a bit too tightly. Dori knew out in the real world that East was strong, but there was never a time that Dori feared him. However, inside his mind, a mind flooded with a curse, Dori found herself nervous about what kind of strength he held.

"Whoa, hey, slow down." Dori tried pulling her hand back, with no luck.

"Can't, they need us to find them. They have been lost for too long." East briskly walked her over to the path, but once they were on the path East froze. He couldn't decide which way to follow it. Dori took a look, but in a move that shouldn't have surprised her, the path she had come down had changed and nothing looked familiar.

"Which way?" East looked at her for answers. She had no idea; this wasn't her brain. But she couldn't exactly tell him that, at least she didn't think she could. Dori should have asked North if she was allowed to tell East that this was a dream. They all agreed she would be his guide, but she never clarified how much she was allowed to tell him in order to point him on the right path. If she told him too much, would the dream they were in dissolve? If it did, what would happen to her?

"What way looks best to you?" Dori asked. Back and forth East kept looking at both options. He would take a step or two one way and then change his mind. Dori tried to think of something she could say to help him. His memories were what the curse took away, but Dori could see it took more than that. He lacked any confidence in his own decision making, self-doubt growing out of control. Dori reached out and grabbed his hand, causing him to stop and look at her.

"Take a breath. One way will lead us where we need to go, and the other will lead us further away. You have an idea on which is which. You just need to look inside and find which way is pulling you closer to your friends."

East looked at her in disbelief, but Dori stepped closer.

"Close your eyes. Take a breath. Listen to that voice inside, what's it telling you?"

Without a second thought East closed his eyes, straightened his back, and started listening to the world around him. Just when Dori thought he was making progress East peeked through one eyelid at her. Without meaning to, Dori rolled her eyes.

"Focus. Focus on the air around us. Focus on the sound of the leaves in the wind. Focus on the feel of my hand in yours. Focus on your gut. What's it telling you?"

East closed his eyes again and really started listening. Dori could feel him twitch his hand against hers every so often, as if to make sure she wasn't going anywhere. After a few moments his eyes popped open and, without uttering a word, he started pulling Dori down the path.

They walked hand in hand, not in any rush, as the path constantly opened up in front of them. The panic and rush from earlier had passed and now the sun was beaming down on them, warming their faces. Dori knew this couldn't go on forever, she understood she was in East's head, but after all the fighting and running for their lives, this quiet moment was one she wasn't ready to give up so quickly.

Looking over at East Dori could almost see the wheel turning in his head. The longer they walked the less afraid he looked and the more at peace he appeared to be. More peace turned into more confidence, and it started to seep out of his body like rays of light seeped out of the sun.

The path itself kept changing as they walked, eventually morphing into a crossroads. Four paths all leading different directions with East and Dori standing right in the middle. East took a moment to look down each road, all of them looking identical to Dori.

"Which way do we go?" she asked quietly, hoping he had an answer.

"They all lead somewhere. Question is, which one leads where we want to go. The path behind us obviously leads back to the field. That's not where they are. That leaves three to choose from. Left, straight, or right." East, still holding on to Dori's hand, closed his eyes, listening to the world around him. The light wind blowing in his face, the high sun keeping them warm. When he opened his eyes, seemingly knowing what to do, he looked right at Dori.

"Thank you," he said graciously. Keeping eye contact with Dori as long as he could, East turned and started walking, leading Dori down the path heading to the left. A few steps in it felt like the world was starting to tip on its axis. Dori stumbled while East kept walking like he didn't notice. His hand left hers and two blinks later Dori sat straight up in the cot, back in reality. North was inches away from her face, a look of concern reflecting in his eyes.

"What happened?" His raspy voice was a strange comfort to her. Dori took a good, long look at his face, before turning to the other side of the cot and vomiting up the entire cup of tea from before.

North started rubbing her back as Elowynn brought over a cool cloth to put on Dori's head. Once her stomach had emptied itself, she looked over at East's cot. He was still lying there, seemingly asleep.

"Why isn't he waking up?" Dori asked, her throat raw. A burst of wind came out of nowhere, traveling across the land, blowing all the candles out. It came from every direction, coming in from every side, until it hit East all at the same time. East's eyes popped open and every person in the room held their breath. There was no way to tell if it worked, if the curse was broken, until he said something.

Something was off with the way he held still. North wasn't going to take any chances, putting himself between East and Dori, in the event that he came back wrong or worse off than before. East's eyes flitted to North's first. A recognition and sense of familiarity and longing struck there. North, taking a deep breath in relief, knew then that Dori had done it.

"East?" West broke the silence as Dori leaned around North to see how East was reacting. West had stepped up to the cots, wringing his hands together, almost scared to hope it worked.

"Not East. Callan." A more serious voice boomed out of him as he sat up slowly, taking a look around, and then stood. It became apparent to everyone around him, just in the way that he was standing, that the unaware, sweet, careful giant from before had transformed back into the warrior that he was meant to be. Callan looked over at Dori.

"I remember you. Not completely, but bits and pieces."

Dori gave him a half smile, hoping the memories were good ones. Not able to stay back anymore, she stepped around North and allowed Callan to take her hands in his.

"You saved me. You helped me. I will forever do what I can to keep any harm from befalling you. My eternal friendship is yours."

Dori, still feeling weak from the tea, almost fell over at the strength coming through his voice. The confidence of a warrior who had been asleep for far too long.

"Hi." Dori didn't know what to say to that, and before she could come up with anything, Callan pulled her forward into an all-encompassing hug. After a few moments he pulled back, looking at the rest of the room.

"So, who wants to tell me the whole story? I have bits and pieces from during the curse, but chunks are missing. How long have I been cursed, and what in the holy fuck are we doing about the Enchantress that put the curse there?"

Dori instantly liked him so much more than before.

Chapter 15

Callan and North had talked most of the night, North filling Callan in on everything he missed. It was strange to watch someone become aware of things that they had lived through but didn't remember. Callan took it all in stride, but Dori could see the way he looked at North and West when they weren't looking. He missed his friends, and while they were technically right in front of him, it was as plain as the nose on his face, he missed who they used to be.

Dori mostly stayed out of the way, keeping on eye on West, who kept falling asleep sitting up against a wall. He refused to be shown a bed he could sleep in, not wanting to be parted from the group for even one moment. The bags around his eyes clearly showed that sleep had been a luxury he didn't allow himself when he was back in the cottage. The constant fear of anything and everything keeping him awake all hours of the night. It was nice for all of them to see West trust them enough to close his eyes knowing they were around to protect him.

The next morning Dori was up early. She couldn't stop replaying the night before in her head. Doing her best to not wake anyone up, Dori quietly walked out of the hut and into the day, only to remember too late how high up she was. During the night she was exhausted enough to forget they weren't on the ground, but now, standing by herself on the walkway in the trees, that initial fear spiked, and Dori's palms started to sweat again.

While it was nice that Elowynn and her people allowed them to stay the night in the safety of the trees, Dori was ready to be back down on earth. Glancing back inside the hut, Dori considered waking someone up to help her climb down the ladder. The only thing that stopped her was the shame and embarrassment she felt about being a bother over something that didn't seem like a big deal to the others.

That only left one option: Dori was going to have to find her own way down. Looking around she noticed that there were a few people coming out of their tents, but for the most part the camp was still asleep.

Dori followed the platform around the tree until it reached the ladder from the night before. No one had used it yet, the ladder itself was still rolled up at the top of the tree platform. Using her foot to push it over the side, Dori heard more than saw it unravel on its way down. Knowing that if she looked down, she would get dizzy immediately, she tried her best to keep her head level and not to let her eyes wander.

One deep breath, two deep breaths. Dori sat on the platform and shuffled herself forward until her legs were hanging off the edge. While it may not have been the best plan, Dori didn't want to think too many steps ahead in case she psyched herself out. Once she started down the ladder, she wouldn't be able to stop halfway if she became terrified. There was also no one at the bottom to catch her if her foot slipped. Wiping her sweaty hands on her pants one last time, Dori took action.

"Okay, here we go. Slow and steady, Dori." Talking to herself was a stress reliever, had been for her entire life. Slowly but smoothly, she turned her body so that she was on her stomach, and then she searched around with her foot for the first rung of the ladder. Her hands were clawing onto the wood boards on the platform, hoping it was enough to keep her in one spot until she was ready.

Both her feet eventually found the ladder and Dori allowed her body to put some weight on it. Slower than she had ever moved in her life Dori lowered herself, one foot at a time, to the next rung on the ladder, and then the next. By this time, she was down far enough that her hands were no longer on the platform, but on the ladder as well.

"Okay, we're okay. We're doing okay, we've got this. Just breath." Still refusing to look down, Dori, in her shaky state, kept moving, one rung at a time. Controlling her breathing, how fast her legs were moving, and how hard her hands were holding on to the ladder, was taking a toll and started draining her energy at an advanced rate.

Dori had made it halfway down before the ladder itself started to sway a bit more. Dori already had sweat trickling down her face, but a last-minute decision to look down to see how far she still had to go had sped her heart up even more.

"Oh, that was stupid, that was a bad idea. Dori, what have you gotten yourself into?" The more she thought about it, the more she ended up shaking the ladder, which caused her to become shakier. It was a vicious circle, and if she didn't start moving again, she was certain she was done for.

"Keep moving, let's go. Was it worth it, huh? Was this worth not having to ask for help? Was this worth proving to a certain someone that you didn't need his help? Because maybe you did. Maybe he would come in handy right about now." The last word squeaked out as her foot slipped for a moment. Getting it back on the rung Dori internally scolded herself and then started moving again.

Finally, Dori had the sense that she was close to the ground, and when she looked, she was only one rung away. Quickly she climbed down the last rung before completely falling onto the grass in relief. She had sweat covering every inch of her body and her arms were shaky from the effort it took to hold onto the ladder.

Laying on the ground, staring up at the sky and the hidden colony of citizens, Dori took a moment to just be calm. The sight itself was a beautiful one, the blue sky, white fluffy clouds, dark green trees. The other sight was just as beautiful. The scene of a people who could not just accept what was happening to the land. The people, the citizens, hiding in the trees would probably be tortured and killed if they were caught, however they were building community despite the horrific conditions they were told to live with. It was a beautiful thing, to see life overcoming even the lowest of odds.

Feeling better, Dori pushed herself up to stand. She could hear running water, a river of some sort had to be nearby. A fresh drink of water was just what she needed after all that exertion. Not thinking much about letting someone know where she was going, Dori took off through the trees and walked until she found a small river flowing. The water looked clean; crystal clear as a matter of fact.

Crouching down and dipping her hand in it, and then sipping the water from the palm of her hand, Dori groaned. She had never tasted anything so pure and delicious. Handful after handful, Dori drank the water until her stomach could hold no more. Dori sat back on her heels and looked around. The riverbank was full of life. Flowers and shrubbery were flourishing, with butterflies and dragonflies flitting about from flower to flower.

A snort made her come to her senses as she turned to her right. Fifty feet in front of her stood a wild boar, and its entire focus was on her. Slowly Dori stood up fully and the heartbeat that she had managed to relax spiked again. In that moment Dori did what she knew she shouldn't have done. She backed away, turned, and started to flee back to camp.

The boar instantly gave chase, moving faster than she expect him to. He was easily a couple hundred pounds, maybe more, and the tusks on him looked sharp enough to puncture a shield, or her rib cage. Her measly skin and bones wouldn't hold up very well, she would be torn to shreds. The deep grunting and snorting was getting closer and closer to her and Dori knew she wouldn't be able to outrun him much longer.

Dori could see camp coming up, but the moment she took her eyes off the ground she tripped over the gnarly root of a tree and face planted into the dirt. Quickly she turned around only to discover the boar had caught up and was getting ready to charge her. Just as Dori thought she was a goner someone jumped over her body and put themselves between her and the boar. West. Handsome, fearful West.

He was standing over her, raising his arms as high as he could, bellowing at the beast, trying to scare it away. In one arm he held a sword and in his other an axe. He was yelling at the boar, mostly grunts and shouts, and stomping his foot every step he took. Dori had never seen West look quite so fierce. He was standing straight up, shoulders puffed out, exuding nothing but confidence and strength. Where was the man who hid behind her in the brawl the other day? Where was the man that hid under a pile of clothing so he wouldn't have to answer his door? He was the fearful caterpillar that had molted into the warrior butterfly.

For a moment it looked like the boar was going to back off and run into the bush, but at the last second it charged West and Dori panicked.

"No!" She jumped to her feet and made to move forward to help when someone pulled her back by the waist and into a solid chest. His scent hit her, and she knew it was North.

"Wait. Just watch," he whispered in her ear, and they both stood there, breathing in sync.

Instead of turning and cowering, the way he had been doing since they had found him, West had turned into the predator. Every time it went to charge West, he would use the sword blade to deflect it as he jumped out of the way. The way West seemed to be able to predict what the boar was going to do reflected to everyone watching that West was playing with the beast. Dori looked away and noticed the crowd they were gathering.

"Shouldn't we help him?" Dori asked North, who just shook his head, not taking his eyes off of West.

"He needs to do this. He needs to know that he can do this." And with that everyone silenced themselves while West worked his way around a boar that was getting more agitated with every missed charge. At last, the boar went right for West and, instead of deflecting it, West ran him through with the sword, followed by taking the axe to the boars' head and in one swing, with a loud roar, severing it from the boar's body.

Cheers rang out from those around them, causing West to look up in shock, as if he didn't know that an audience was watching. There he stood, out of breath and covered in boar blood spatter, taking the moment in. A second later, with a smile on his face, West picked up the bloody axe and raised it in the air as a sign of triumph.

That's when Dori noticed the glowing. Starting at the tip of his head a glowing light flowed through his body, ending in the hand that held the axe. Less than a second later the ground shook and a pulse of energy came off him.

The crowd went silent again as they watched the once cowardly man stand up straighter and raise his chin a little higher.

His eyes found Dori and he gave her the largest, most genuine smile as he ran at her. Dori, slightly surprised, went to back up only to find North was still holding on to her.

When he reached her North gave her a little push and West picked her up in a bear hug, twirling her around. Dori couldn't stop the giggle that came out of her mouth.

"Whoa, West …"

He stopped twirling and slowly put her down. Looking into his eyes Dori could see the relief and happiness flooding in. He looked slightly bashful once he realized what he had just done. Holding his hands up in a nonthreatening manner, he couldn't hold back his smile.

"Sorry, sorry. Oh, and not West. Gunner. Fucking Gunner! Yeah, man! Fuck that curse! Feels so good to be on this side!" Gunner let out a victorious shout that echoed off the trees. His excitement was contagious and everyone around him started letting out their own victorious shouts, North being one of the loudest. Two curses broken; it was only a matter of time before they took the Enchantress down.

Dori looked at North. North, the warrior, still stuck behind a curse that kept his true power away from him. On the outside he was celebrating, but Dori could see it. His smile, not quite reaching his eyes. His refusal to look straight at anyone, instead looking up as he cheered. The light inside of him flickering as hope slowly drained from him. There was something bugging him, Dori could see it. Watching two guardians beat the odds, leaving him alone on the other side of things.

Heartbreak and loneliness, that's what Dori saw, and looking around it was clear that she was the only one that saw it.

Chapter 16

Celebration was in the air. There was a sense of hope, joyful laughter could be heard, and in response the songs of the beautiful birds echoed back towards the group. It almost felt as if the land surrounding them was able to take a deep breath for the first time in years.

The grass she stood on felt lusher and the leaves on the trees surrounding them were swaying gently in the breeze. The sun was setting, and the sky was turning into the most spectacular deep blue fading into black. The stars were starting to shine, and Dori stood there, staring at it all with nothing less than awe.

The smell of the bonfire, the stars in the sky, even the flowers along the trail that Dori was admiring earlier, all of it seemed to be beaming. Whatever hold the Enchantress had on the land was starting to slip and Dori hoped she could do even more good before she had to go.

Lighthearted laughter could be heard around her as food and drink were being passed out and enjoyed. The mood of the entire encampment was a happy one. Mostly happy, with one exception. Dori shifted her focus to the image across the bonfire, where she saw North sitting alone, tucked away by bushes, his back to the crowd. Dori stepped around the bonfire, weaving around people, making her way to the large rock that North was perched on.

At first, she didn't say anything as she climbed up to sit beside him. He was looking out across a clearing, seemingly staring at the stars as night started to bloom. The crackling of the fire behind them combined with the chirping of crickets made this moment almost impossibly perfect. The night chill started seeping in as Dori pulled her jacket a bit tighter around herself.

"You should go back to the fire," North grunted, still refusing to look at her. His body was radiating tension, the tone in his voice was strained. With everything turning in their favor, North should have been at least slightly less perturbed. Yet, it was almost as if he was being dragged down further at the sight of happiness that he couldn't reach.

"I'm okay," Dori responded. The chill of the night wasn't enough to chase her away from someone who's soul, who's entire being was obviously aching. North had been hot and cold with her since day one, and yet she couldn't force herself to stop caring about his wellbeing.

"I have no doubt you're okay. You're always okay. But you are also cold, so you should go back to the fire." He held an edge in his voice. Trying to push her away yet again, it was becoming a pattern with North. In the beginning she may have listened and back away. Not anymore. Not after what they had been through together. It would take more than a few curt words to chase her away. If nothing else, Dori believed him to be her friend, and he was hurting. Alone was the last thing he needed to be.

"I don't want to. I want to stay here, sitting beside you."

He aggressively sighed at that. The two of them sat there, in silence, for a few more minutes. The cheerful banter happening behind them around the fire was a stark contrast to the two of them, sitting side by side on the rock, tension building until Dori couldn't stay quiet anymore.

"Do you want to talk about it?" Dori asked. She didn't clarify what she was asking him about, but he knew that somehow, despite the fact that he hadn't said a thing, she knew exactly what was bothering him. He didn't really want to discuss anything, but was also finding it hard to brush her off.

The last few days had completely changed his world. Not just because the fight seemed to be turning in their favor, but because this woman, who appeared out of nowhere, was everything he never thought possible in one person. The kind heart, the smart brain, the resilience in the face of complete asshole-ness. Dori kept surpassing every notion he held about her, and it wasn't something he knew how to deal with. Ignoring her wasn't working, and North had a feeling that she would sit there all night in silence if she needed to.

The coming days were going to be hard, he understood that this opportunity may be the last time he was able to talk to her alone. They weren't on the run, they weren't in the middle of a brawl, prying eyes and ears were all busy with something else, and there was no goal to reach. It had turned into a now or never situation. Taking a deep breath and letting it out slowly, North started talking.

"What ... what if my curse can't be broken?"

It wasn't the words that brought a tear to Dori's eyes, but the silent plea hidden within it. North didn't want to be cold and distant for the rest of his existence. Watching everyone celebrate together, laugh together, it had become obvious to Dori that North didn't have it in him to fully join in. He could pretend, put on a mask and almost no one would notice the dull light in his eyes while he was doing it. But Dori took notice.

"We'll find a way." Dori truly believed it. There was nothing they couldn't do as a group, and the list of allies kept growing. They wouldn't stop until every curse was broken. Every blade of grass would feel the sun again, every imprisoned person would be freed. North scoffed at her perfectly positive answer.

"How do you make a guy without a heart feel something other than bitter despair?" Still refusing to look her way, North looked up at the sky, seeing the beauty that it held and not feeling a thing about it. It was empty, his chest, and with no heart the beauty of the world just didn't amaze him the way it used to. He truly believed that if he were to bang on his chest, he would hear an empty echo.

"I don't believe that, you know. That you don't have a heart. I know for a fact you do." Dori's sweet voice floated through his ears and down his spine. He wanted so badly to believe what she was saying.

"I've been cursed, Dori. I think that's obvious."

Her optimism was admirable, but the sooner Dori realized there was a chance he couldn't be saved the better it would be for her in the end. He didn't want to give her false hope, especially since he knew her heart would be broken in the end when it turned out she couldn't fix him.

"I'm not saying you haven't been cursed. I just don't think the curse worked the way you've been led to believe. I believe the curse powered down your heart, if that makes sense."

A curse was a curse, in North's eyes. The specifics meant nothing if overall it meant that he couldn't feel all of the important emotions. How was he going to get Dori to understand that?

"How is that any better?" Logic versus hopeful thinking, a battle that was waged throughout the ages. North knew his heart was broken, or dead. It didn't matter how she wanted to describe it.

"Not having a heart at all is an impossible mountain to climb. But having one that just needs a jump start, that is something attainable. Besides, I've seen evidence of your heart." There wasn't one ounce of uncertainty in her voice. Not for one single moment did she hesitate. Dori believed what she said, and even if she was wrong, that belief meant the world to North.

"You have not." North could barely come up with one example of him not being an insufferable asshole. What Dori was trying to suggest, there was no way it was true.

"Yes, I have, the first day I met you. I knew then and there you still had a heart." Dori tilted her face towards North, trying desperately to get him to look at her. If he just looked at her, he would see the belief she had in him in her eyes. North was a fickly man, and a stubborn one at that. He still refused to look at her.

"You mean the day I shot at you and East, trying to drive you away from the property?" Had that only been a few days prior? Time was moving faster than he would have liked.

"Yes. That's part of it. You shot at us." Dori finished the sentence in a full smile, as she recalled running and ducking with East, pieces of trees flying past them as his bullets hit anything but his targets.

"Exactly, I was trying to hurt you. People with hearts don't try to hurt others." North stood up from the rock and took a few steps away to get some space, putting his hands in his pockets.

"North, you're the best marksman of the group. You were shooting at two of the most uncoordinated fools in this land. If you had wanted to hit us, to hurt us, it would have taken two bullets and that's it. If you had wanted to hurt us, you would have." North turned in her direction, slightly stunned. There she sat on a giant boulder, shaking from the cold, and yet full of confidence and belief. Belief in him.

"You also stood up for East when you first met me, you attacked a member of the Enchantress's guard when you thought I was in danger, you forced us to travel through the night to make sure your other friend, who couldn't defend himself, was alright, and when you saw what had happened to him you went into a rage because you wanted to protect him. Go on, tell me I'm lying." The fierceness on her face, the utter belief she had in him, was breathtaking. He still didn't want to believe it, to accept it. Couldn't she just let him be miserable and hopeless? At least then there wouldn't be disappointment when curing him failed.

"Well, if I have a heart then why hasn't the curse cracked yet?"

The absolute vulnerability flooding out of that question took Dori by surprise. There was a part of him that was scared, and animals that were scared would run or hide.

"Maybe it was never about you growing a heart. Maybe it's about you admitting that you have one, and putting your faith in what it makes you feel." It was a theory Dori had, a theory she hoped was true.

"I don't even know what that means." North threw his arms in the air in utter frustration. Nothing was ever easy, nothing was ever simple when it came to curses.

"It means don't push everyone away all the time. Join the bonfires once in a while. Let the kids tell you corny jokes. Get invested in others. I noticed that you haven't talked to Callan or Gunner much, other than updating them, since their curses were broken. Not a real, in-depth conversation. The closest you came was the night Callan's curse broke, and even then, from what I heard, you mostly updated him like he was a solider in your army. You talked about facts, but not once did you discuss how you felt throughout the last ten years."

How dare she assume to know what was going through his mind at any time?

"I don't have anything to say to them. They aren't on the same journey anymore." North shook his head and turned away from Dori again, looking out at the horizon and trying to dismiss her. Brick by brick Dori could see North building those walls again. She would be damned if she let him just board himself back up at this point, for all eternity. Curses couldn't be broken if the cursed person didn't believe that there could be salvation on the other side of the pain and torment.

"They may not be on the same journey anymore, but they're still on the same damn map as you." Infuriated, Dori jumped off the rock and went to stand by North, grabbing his arm and turning him towards her. North glanced in her eyes and then tried to stop himself from doing it again. It was hard to lie straight to her face. Impossible, even.

"It just makes me angry. I'm happy that they both were able to rid themselves of their curses. But now they look at me as if I'm the damsel in distress. Poor North can't remember his own name and is being controlled by someone that we never should have lost to in the first place!" Once he started speaking the truth, it was as if the dam broke. He couldn't contain it anymore; all of his inner thoughts started leaking out faster than he could contain them. Dori's eyes turned softer, not out of pity, but compassion.

"They just want to help you." Her voice was barely a whisper. North exploded in anger and frustration, causing Dori to jump back for a moment as he pulled his arms away.

"No! No one helps me! I help others! I help them! I help stupid East who doesn't understand when he's being taken advantage of, and I help pathetic West who can't even leave his house because of how scared he is! I do the helping; I don't need the helping!" Tears started filling North's eyes as he was desperately trying to blink them back. Waves of emotion started washing over him, each one more intense than the one before.

"Do you think they'll see you any differently if you simply ask for help? Do you really think it weakens you in their eyes?" Dori kept her voice soft but filled it with strength. North spoke, his eyes locked onto hers.

"I don't give two shits about how they perceive me! I lasted the past ten years just fine. I'm happy their lives have been fixed, but they aren't the ones I care about right now!" That stopped Dori for a moment. How did they go from talking about his close group of friends to someone else. Confused, Dori responded.

"Well then, who is winding you into such a little prick?" She didn't mean to swear at him, but at this point Dori had no filter. The emotions swirling throughout the air were starting to overtake her common sense and verbal filters. North took three intimidating steps towards her, all the while shouting at her.

"You! You are! I don't want you to see me as weak, as someone who can't take care of things!" All the air left Dori's lungs. Out of everything she expected North to be angry about, her opinion of him was at the very bottom of that list.

"Why not?" Dori let him step closer, not fearing for her safety for one moment. She knew North would never hurt her, no matter how frustrated or infuriated he was about any given situation. She felt completely safe with him.

"Because how am I supposed to get you to agree to stay with me if you don't think I can take care of you!" North shouted at her.

Dori stood there, staring into the most beautiful ice blue eyes, emotionally stunned at what he was saying.

"I ... I didn't think you even liked me." Dori's palms started sweating, this wasn't what she expected when she woke up that morning. This wasn't what she expected ever, and yet this beautiful behemoth of a man was concerned with her opinion of him. Life was strange most days, but this day really took the cake.

"Of course I like you! You are the kindest human I've ever met! You're courageous, you stand up for people you don't even know just because it's the right thing to do! You're fucking beauty overwhelms me, inside and out! Just looking at you is like witnessing a shooting star! It's a miracle to me that someone like you exists! You are everything I've ever wanted and everything I'm terrified of losing before I have the chance to–" Dori threw herself at North, lips crashing as tears fell from her eyes like raindrops during a storm. His hands gripped at her face, holding her to him with the grip of someone who was one misstep away from falling off a cliff. Dori grabbed the lapels of his jacket, tugging his body right close to hers, holding on as hard as she could, as if he would float away at the slightest breeze.

A crack echoed throughout the sky as if the universe had finally aligned in its truest form. The crack was followed by the night sky being flooded with bright, vivid greens, purples, and reds. The curse on North was broken, the land was healing, the dancing lights had returned.

Not that Dori or North noticed right away. They were still wrapped up in each other. That is until they heard the collective gasps, shouts, and cheers. Dori's first thought was that everyone must have been looking at them, and embarrassment flooded her cheeks. Both her and North looked at the crowd behind them at the same time before noticing that no one was looking at them, because everyone was pointing up into the sky.

Dori looked up at the colors floating above them and started to full on sob and laugh at the same time. North looked up and let his entire face melt into the most gracious smile. Tears filled his eyes as he let out his own victorious shout.

The land was alive and was letting them know. It was ready to fight, it was time for a fight. North looked back down at Dori and vowed that, whatever it took, he would not let anything happen the woman that brought back the dancing lights. He pulled her focus back to him and kissed her again. He grabbed her hand and, after one more quick kiss, led her to the bonfire, where everyone was stomping, clapping, hooting and hollering, and dancing. North started leading Dori in a dance, letting her twirl away only to pull her back, smiling at her carefree laugh and the light dancing in her eyes.

After pulling her back in a third time he brushed his lips against her ear.

"Rune," he said quietly, knowing that, despite all the noise around him she would hear him. Dori froze and looked up at him before whispering back.

"I told you your heart was in there. Rune."

He smiled back at her and picked her up around the waist in a hug.

Chapter 17

The night was settling in as most of the celebrations were winding down and most celebrators had stumbled their way up the ladders and into their beds. The sky above was crystal clear, stars twinkling and a light warm wind weaving in and out of the trees.

Callan, Gunner, Rune, and Dori remained, seated around what remained of the campfire. The embers were still hot, but the flames were on their last legs. Dori had watched the three men embrace after Rune had broken his curse. His face looked different and yet the same all at once. Most of the sadness and rage had left his face. His memories and his strength were returning.

Callan and Gunner had given her giant hugs when they discovered Rune's curse had been broken. Since that moment the three of them stood together, gossiping like schoolgirls. They would include Dori in what they could, and Rune would constantly look over to silently check in with her. Dori had never been the high maintenance kind, so she found a log close enough to the fire to keep her warm, and then she sat down and enjoyed watching the people around her come to life.

The morale of the rebels was at an all-time high, at least in the small amount of time that she had been there. Watching the joy on their faces as they danced around the three oblivious men in the middle, their guardians were coming back to them and the relief and hope they felt was contagious.

Slowly, as the night wore on, small groups of people left for bed, exhausted by the celebrations. Callan, Gunner, and Rune had made their way to tree stumps by Dori, still talking amongst each other. Eventually the talk slowed down and now the four of them were watching the flames dancing and dwindling. Dori was starting to wonder how difficult the last curse would be to break. The fact that Elowynn hadn't mentioned it again had Dori wondering if she really knew how to help South.

As if Elowynn had read her mind, Elowynn appeared from behind one of the trees and gracefully walked over to the group. Her eyes staring Dori down as she walked towards them.

"You have questions about the fourth curse." She made her way to stand between Rune and Dori, putting a hand on each of them as she softly spoke.

"The only reason we were able to break these three curses was because I was in direct contact with them. I don't think I'll be able to get near enough to South. And I have no idea how to even go about breaking the curse. I just, I don't see the way forward from here." Callan, Rune, and Gunner all grunted their agreement. Elowynn smiled down at Dori.

"The curse on South isn't quite the same as the others. The curse placed upon your friend is poppy based. It's one of the strongest curses my sister could have placed upon him. The fact that she is constantly strengthening the curse is also a problem. There is no way to break this curse without magical intervention."

"So, what? There's no way to save him?" Rune's gruff voice caused Dori's heart to drop. There had to be a way to save South. She was brought from another world to do this. Elowynn turned to Rune.

"There is one way to save him, but it will take more effort." Elowynn's voice drifted into the quiet night. "South is buried by the curse. He won't be able to get out of it on his own. Dori, your presence is still important, but it's also not enough on its own. What South needs is a counter-curse. You'll need to gather a specific set of ingredients and a sacred incantation. Only when all of these things are brought together will South have a chance at breaking free."

"Well, alright. Let's start gathering these ingredients. Let's get him out of there." Callan stood up, ready to leave immediately. But Elowynn lifted her hand, telling him to be patient.

"It will be a dangerous journey. These ingredients aren't very accessible. And even if you manage to collect all three and the incantation, you have to be standing in the same room as him when you put it together. My sister won't take kindly to intruders, and she is the type to shoot first and ask questions later. You need to ask yourselves if you are prepared to give your all for South. You might get hurt, or worse."

Dori took a moment to breath. It was easy to sit around and talk about taking the Enchantress down. The reality of it was that she was extremely powerful, and she had the upper hand. While Dori wouldn't hesitate to jump in and help, she was becoming very aware that helping could lead to getting hurt. Gunner was the next to speak, his low voice cracking at first.

"He would do it for us. He would go to the ends of the earth for us, if it meant we would have a chance at being free. He would do it for us." Rune stood, walking toward him and nodding in agreement, while Callan slapped his shoulder in a show of solidarity. All three men looked over at Dori, who looked up at Elowynn.

"What are the ingredients we need to collect?" Dori asked her.

Elowynn smiled once again.

"To break South's poppy curse, you'll need to melt the snow from the top of the highest mountain. Add to that the hair of an equine touched with magic. The last thing you'll need, and the hardest to acquire, is the ash from a burning witch's broom. Combine those three things, drop in the emerald that travelled between worlds, say the incantation three times while in the same room as South. The curse will break, and your friend will be free." The list sounded almost impossible.

How would they even know if a horse was touched by magic? And did they really need to climb a mountain for a bit of snow? This was madness. Then again, as Dori was learning, madness thrived here.

"What's the incantation?" Dori asked. Elowynn reached into a hidden pocket and pulled out a small vial, filled with a piece of paper, a small cork keeping it sealed.

"When the time is right, take this out and read it." She handed it over to Dori. As Dori went to take it from her hands, Elowynn reached out with her other hand and enclosed it over top of Dori's hand, effectively holding her in place. Dori's gaze snapped up to Elowynn's.

"Complete these tasks, break this curse, and you'll be saving our lands and our people. Fail, and we'll all be doomed to live this life until the end of our days."

Dori felt immense pressure pushing down on her shoulders as she pulled her hand back, the small vial within it.

"We leave at first light. Gentlemen let's get a bit of sleep. We're going to need it." With that they disbanded, putting the fire out and climbing up the rope ladders to the last safe place they would be sleeping for a while.

Rune helped Dori make it to the top, and once she was on the platform she took a small moment alone to look out at the horizon. A warm wind whipped around her, starting at her toes and traveling up until it brushed her hair out of her face.

"We're coming for you, South. Just please hold on," Dori whispered into the wind, before turning and finding a spot to sleep for the last few hours of the night.

Chapter 18

Early the next morning the four of them woke up to find a bag for each of them packed with an extra set of clothes, a full waterskin, and a small amount of food. It would seem that they were alone on the platforms, the others having started their regular patrolling routines. After a quick wash up and a small breakfast they were all ready to go.

Walking up to the rope ladder, Dori instantly frowned. It was the worst part of living in the trees, and she wasn't prepared to go back down it yet again. This time, with 3 warrior guardians there to witness her cowardness, it was bound to be humiliating.

"Climb on." Rune's deep voice startled her from behind. She turned to look at him with confusion written all over her face.

"Don't rush me." Dori went to turn back around when Rune grabbed her arm to stop her.

"Not the ladder. Me. Climb on." Instantly Dori felt her face turn bright red, but she didn't have time to think about what he meant before Rune had turned around and knelt down, giving her access to his back and shoulders.

"How are you going to climb down the ladder if I'm hanging off of you. We'll fall."

Callan and Gunner stood to the side, pretending to strap their packs to themselves, but smirking at the display in front of them.

"Woman, the curse is broken. My strength is fully back. My agility, my balance, it's at an all-time high. Trust me when I say climbing down with you on my back isn't the challenge you think it is. Now climb on before I have the others strap you on there."

Dori glanced over at Callan, who just nodded at her. Dori turned back and walked up to his back. Slowly she placed her arms over his shoulders, locking her hands in front of his neck. Her knees instinctively lifted up; her feet unable to lock around his stomach due to the size of him.

With Dori completely hanging off of Rune like a baby monkey, Rune pushed himself backwards until his legs hung off of the platform. Dori squeaked and her stomach dropped, and she was about to tell him to put her down before she vomited all over his back. But she wasn't quick enough, and with more speed and agility than she gave him credit for, Rune was climbing down the ladder at record speed. In less than a minute they were on the ground, safely. Dori forced her hands to let go, as she slid her body down his back, until her feet hit the ground. Rune turned around and grasped her chin, tilting it up so he could look in her eyes.

"Told you." He dropped a kiss to her forehead before moving her out of the way so that the other two could come down. Dori had to sit down for a minute, her head spinning at the feelings brewing up inside of her.

With the four of them on the ground, Callan pointed the way to the mountain, and they were off on the next part of their journey.

"What's so special about this snow anyway?"

They had been walking for hours, with no sign that an end was in sight. There were mountains in the distance, but Dori couldn't tell which one they were aiming for. She also couldn't conceive how far up the mountain they would have to hike up. While she was appreciative to still have Rune's extra clothing, the boots she wore weren't equipped for her feet to go up a mountain. Dori could already feel the blisters that would form on that hike.

Gunner walked up beside her, handing her a waterskin to take a sip of. The three men seemed to be taking turns taking care of her. Less than an hour ago Callan pulled two apples out of his bag and, walking past her, placed one in her hands, while Rune had twice now stopped her to make sure she was drinking enough water.

Now that all three of them were back to normal they were taking the guardian role and running with it. While Dori appreciated that they cared, she was a full-grown adult and could decide when she needed a sip of water. Gunner waited until she drank from the waterskin before answering her question.

"Legend has it snow from the top of this mountain, when applied to the eyes of someone under the poppy spell, has been known to 'wake' the person from eternal sleep. At least that's what the people of the forest claim." Gunner's voice, while deep like Callan and Rune, had a smoothness to it. Dori could have listened to him talk for hours on end. He took the waterskin back and placed it in his bag.

"How far away is the mountain we're looking for?" Dori needed a goal, at least something to work towards. The sun was up, the day was hot, and the last thing she wanted to do was walk through the muggy forest for a few more hours.

"We're closer than it looks. The land will start to slope soon. You'll be walking up the base of the mountain without even knowing it. We should be there by mid-afternoon. If we're quick enough we can have the snow and be back at the base by the time the moon is high in the sky."

Dori's mouth dropped open.

"Wait, we're walking down the mountain at night?" Not only were Dori's legs shaking at the thought of walking that long, but what about the wild animals that came out once the sun went down?

"Don't worry, Dori. We'll keep you safe." Gunner smiled at her, his confidence radiating out towards her. When he saw the look on her face, the hesitation, he responded quietly.

"We normally would take more breaks, maybe a slower pace, but it's hard knowing our friend is trapped. We don't know what hell she's putting him through. Now that all three of us are fully aware of everything, we want him out of there as soon as we can. If it was possible for us to walk for days on end without a break, we would. He's our family." Gunner gave Dori an apologetic smile before moving on. Dori understood where they were coming from and started feeling guilty at wanting to complain about their pace.

Although their constant need to fuel her up without stopping made more sense now that she had a better understanding of how urgent this was to them. Less than an hour later Dori saw the start of a trail up ahead. With her eyes following where it started curving, Dori could see the land starting to rise up. They had made it to base of the mountain.

"Let's take a small rest here before we start the trail." Rune spoke to everyone, yet only had eyes for her. His intense stare was assessing her from top to bottom, taking in how much she had slowed down and how worn down she had looked. Dori didn't argue and took two steps to a large rock and sat down. Slipping the boots off to massage her feet felt glorious.

Callan went around, passing out chunks of bread and hard cheese to everyone. Dori ate it so fast she didn't even taste it. Chasing it down with few large gulps of water, her body seemed much more satisfied. The others each found their own spot to rest, Rune's just happened to be across from her. They hadn't talked much since they left that morning, and even now he preferred watching her from a distance.

There were so many words left unsaid between the two of them, but now wasn't the time to sit down and hash it all out. Just sitting across from him, Dori could feel the electricity bouncing between her and Rune.

After everyone rested their feet for a bit, Rune stood up and started getting his pack back on. Everyone took that as an unspoken decision, it was time to make it up the mountain.

As they followed the trail leading them up the mountain Dori took in her surroundings. The dense forest was starting to thin out and the trail was starting to incline at a healthy rate. Looking at the those around her she noticed she was the only one breathing as hard as she was. Every time Dori tried to slow her pace down, the conversation she had with Gunner would pop back into her head. There was very little time to waste.

While lost in her thoughts Dori's foot caught on a tree root, sending her to the ground with a loud grunt. The three men, who were all ahead of her, stopped and turned back. Embarrassment flooded her cheeks as she tried to jump back up.

"I'm fine. I'm okay," Dori tried reassuring them as Rune strutted towards her, kneeling down to look at her knee. Dori looked down to see what he was doing, only to discover a rip in her pants and a gash on her knee.

"Oh, just a scratch."

Rune looked up at her in disagreement, as he took his pack off and rummaged through it. He pulled a piece of cloth out along with his waterskin, wetting the cloth and pressing it to Dori's wound. Rune looked at the other two.

"Time for a break." Both nodded at him in agreement. The embarrassment Dori was feeling grew tenfold.

"No, let's keep going. I'm okay."

Rune grunted at her as he stood up and escorted her to a fallen log, making sure she sat down on it before kneeling back down and cleaning out her wound.

"If you need us to take a break, or slow our pace, you need to say something. And before you argue with me, I can hear how out of breath you are. And now you're tripping over roots trying to keep up." Knowing that he could hear how hard it had become for her to keep up with them filled her with shame. Rune, once again showing how attuned he was with her, shut those thoughts down.

"Don't you dare feel bad about it. We go your pace, not the other way around." Dori sighed at him, not sure if she wanted to voice her thoughts. The way Rune stopped what he was doing and stared her down told her to just say what was on her mind.

"South can't afford for us to slow down. We have to get him out of there."

Rune finished cleaning the wound and sat back on his heels.

"It's true, South needs us. But what happens if we wear ourselves out trying to get there as quickly as we can? What kind of fighting shape are we going to be in? South needs us, and quickly. But he also needs us in top fighting shape if we're going to even have a shot at getting him out." What Rune was saying had logic behind it, but Dori's heart ached for every slow step she needed to take.

"Break's over. Dori, you're leading this time." No one argued with Rune, and that is how Dori ended up hiking up a mountain with three fae guardians trailing behind her.

The air started cooling off quickly and frost was starting to coat the branches on the trees and the blades of grass. The weather shifted quickly and, before she knew it, there were small patches of snow gathering around them.

Trying not to be the weakest link, Dori did her best to hide her shivering from the others. Her clothes weren't exactly meant for snowy weather, but that was no one's fault and there was nothing she could do about it now. Pulling her coat into her neck, Dori placed her hands deep in her pockets and told herself that if she kept moving, she'd be alright. Her nose was bright red, as were her cheeks and the tips of her ears. She was grinding her teeth to keep the chattering at bay, and it took all her energy to act like nothing was bothering her. She was spending so much energy acting like she wasn't freezing, that she didn't notice when Rune approached her from behind.

In typical Rune fashion, he didn't say a thing when he walked by her. He simply placed his jacket on her shoulders. Dori looked at him in shock, and her rejection was on her lips but the look in his eyes told her he wasn't going to take no for an answer. Dori gave him a grateful smile, slipping her arms into his overly large, but warm sleeves. Immediately the muscles in her back and arms started to relax from the warmth.

Once he was assured that she was settled into the jacket Rune turned and kept walking forward. Callan walked up, bumping into Dori's shoulder in a friendly gesture. He smirked at her, glancing ahead at Rune and then back at her, mischief shining in his eyes.

"Shut up," was all she could say as a grin spread across her face. It was like having a little brother tease her for the boy next door coming around. Callan gave a small chuckle.

"Well, who would have thought … that's interesting." And with that he caught up to Rune. Dori grumbled at him under her breath, but took comfort in the extra jacket, and the surly man it came from.

A few moments later Gunner ran up ahead and let out a celebratory shout. He bent down and then quickly turned around, throwing a small snowball at Callan. Callan, not one to be out done, ran towards Gunner and tackled him to the ground.

Laughing at their antics, Dori caught up and saw a few inches of snow covering the ground in front of her. She took her hand out of her pocket and reached down to scoop up a small amount of the crisp, cool snow. Her fingers burned as she held it, letting her body heat melt the snowflakes touching her skin.

Rune walked a few feet away from the rest of the group, pulling a small jar out of his bag and taking the lid off of it. Using the lid, Rune filled the jar to the top with snow, pushing in more and more until it was packed full. He replaced the lid, put the jar in his bag, and then turned to Dori.

"First item acquired." Dori smiled at him before she was hit in the back with a snowball. Loud laughs echoed behind her as she turned to see Callan proudly standing there, with another snowball in his hand.

"Do you take anything seriously?" Rune asked him, only being partially serious.

"Only when I need to." The grin on Callan's face, the pure joy he was experiencing was something Rune didn't think he would ever see his friend experience again. Dori laughed, adding more easiness to the situation, before she scooped up her own snow, throwing it towards Callan. For a few minutes they allowed themselves to enjoy the lightness of the moment. Throwing snowballs at each other eased a bit of the tension and improved everyone's mood.

A half an hour later it was decided that they should start down the mountain, stopping to build a small camp a few hours in to warm up and rest.

Chapter 19

It wasn't until mid-morning the next day that they fully made it down the mountain. Dori's legs, feet, arms everything was sore from sleeping on the ground and all the shivering that happened. Gunner and Callan seemed to be in decent moods as they made it to warmer weather.

"Let me get this straight. Not only did we have to hike up that monstrosity for less that a snowballs worth of snow, but now we must track a random horse through the forest to get a hair from its tail?" Dori finally asked what the hair of an equine touched with magic meant, and after she got her answer there was a part of her that wished she didn't ask at all.

"Not just any horse. And it wasn't just any snow." Rune's husky voice was starting to get snippy with her. Dori knew the travel days had been long and all he could think about was the friend he left behind. Even though he was the one who told her to not wear herself out, Dori could tell that Rune was feeling frustrated about the situation. Callan walked up, putting a hand on Dori's shoulder.

"Magic doesn't always make sense, Dori. Especially not in our land. There are things you still haven't seen that would make could make your brain melt. Figuratively, of course." The way he said it, with such acceptance of things just being off kilter, grated on Dori's nerves.

"I think I liked you more before you started talking about brain melting magic." Callan smirked at her, reaching out to ruffle her hair. Dori swatted at his arm, like she would to an annoying younger brother.

They were coming into a clearing, the blue sky acting as a canvas against the symphony of green plants and grasses, for one of the most incredible sights Dori had ever seen. Stopping just after crossing the edge, Dori felt a small tremor in the ground. Rune came up behind her fast, grabbed her hand and started pulling her over to a set of trees. Once they made it to the trees Rune dropped her hand, but put his arm around her waist and pulled her close to him.

"What are you doing?" Dori asked, confused.

"Moving you out of the way, wouldn't want you to get trampled." His breath tickled the shell of her ear, and for a moment time seemed to pause as Dori looked up into his eyes. The ice blue crystals staring back at her held so much power, it was almost as if she could see the crackling of lightening within. Another tremor came from the ground and Dori used it as a distraction, looking down at her feet.

"What is that?" In an instant a horse came bursting out of the trail to her left. It was galloping at full speed, and before Dori could even take a breath it was followed by another, and another. A herd of horses ran by then. Callan and Gunner all found safe spots to be, climbing trees so as to not spook the horses.

"Holy shit." Dori counted fifteen before she couldn't keep up. They were wild horses, running together as one unit. While beautiful, that wasn't the most impressive thing about them.

Each and every horse had what looked like bioluminescence shimmering on their coats. As the light of day hit them differently the most amazing colors were shining off them. Purples turned into greens, turning into oranges and right into reds. Dori rubbed at her eyes, not believing what she was seeing.

"An equine touched with magic," Dori whispered more to herself than anyone else. Rune hadn't been able to look away from her, his eyes taking in every inch of her face.

"We like to call them a horse of a different color, but yes." His voice was low as he answered her.

Dori let loose the biggest smile she had.

"This feels like a dream." Dori was hesitant to take her eyes off of the animals, the pure wild strength and raw beauty of the beasts almost bringing her to tears.

"How are they still here with all of the curses floating around?"

"My best guess? The forest itself has been using a type of magic to protect what it could. It would take tremendous strength and concentration for the sisters to get their hands on this herd. That's energy they do not have to spare, not now anyways. The last time I saw this herd they were maybe half what they are now. But now, seeing how their numbers have grown, and how healthy they are, it's a clear message that nature is fighting back. It's getting stronger, it's coming back. And that, Dori, is at least in a small part thanks to you."

Dori looked from the horses to Rune. His breath mixing with hers due to their closeness.

"I haven't done anything much, though." Other than mind walking, Dori really had just been in the right place at the right moment.

"Your heart is pure. You set out to help people. That type of kindness comes with its own magic vibrations. Nature is all around us, don't think for a second it doesn't feel the goodness in your heart. It's responding to it, right in front of your face."

Rune reached around Dori and picked a small flower, bringing it up to her face and tucking it behind her ear. The whinnying of horses caused Dori to look back and the herd itself was running into the sunset.

Her voice caught in her throat slightly when she asked Rune "How do we get the hair we need?" Looking up at him she noticed his attention had been taken from her to something over her shoulder. Turning her head Dori inhaled in shock.

Standing ten feet from them was one of the horses, glittering in the sunlight.

"Careful. It's still a wild animal." Rune let Dori slowly turn her body so that she was facing the beast. The other two guardians stayed as still as they could, not making a sound. The horse stomped its front hoof twice, trying to relay a message.

"Is it mad that we're here?" Dori whispered over her shoulder to Rune.

"No. Just the opposite, I think. He wants to help. They know why we're here. If they wanted us gone, they could have stayed hidden. He's here to give us what we need," Rune whispered back.

"Oh. Okay. How exactly are we supposed to get a hair from his mane?" Dori watched the stallion watch her back.

"Walk up to him, I suppose, and pluck one out." Rune said it like it was an everyday occurrence, walking up to a wild horse and pulling its hair.

"That curse must have really fried your circuits," Dori muttered.

"Fried my what?" He glanced at the side of her face, confused at the term.

"I'm saying, you must have lost your mind. He's a wild stallion, who's going to walk up and pluck a hair from him? Who's going to take that chance?"

Rune let a beat of silence past before answering.

"You are. And stop, before you disagree, just listen."

Dori took a breath.

"Okay, I'm listening."

Rune rolled his eyes.

"Not to me. To him. To the birds. To the trees. Nature is talking to you, just listen, and you'll know what to do."

It didn't escape her notice that the advice Rune was giving her sounded very similar to what she told Callan while mind walking.

If she had learned anything being here, it was that trusting her gut had gotten her to this point. It would be foolish to ignore it now. Slowly stepping away from Rune's touch, despite the comfort it gave her, allowed Dori to ground herself in the moment. Closing her eyes Dori let the sun beat down on her face. She felt the wind twist through the strands of her hair. She could hear birds in the distance and leaves in the trees were making their own kind of music. The smell of damp earth and fresh air invaded her spirit. Content, welcomed, and loved, Dori had never felt so accepted before.

Slowly she opened her eyes and made eye contact with the stallion. He shifted his weight in a calm manner, never taking his eyes off her, and Dori knew instantly what she had to do.

Taking slow, steady steps, Dori walked toward the stallion with one hand out. Rune, Callan, and Gunner shifted their weight, ready to jump in just in case the animal wasn't receptive to what Dori was trying to do.

Step by step, Dori got closer, until her hand was hovering over the stallion's velvet nose. She kept it here, letting the stallion make the final move, which he did. He lifted his nose until it hit Dori's hand, showing her it was okay to touch him. She took a deep breath and started petting his nose, moving to his side and dragging her hand through his mane. the colors up close were surreal, almost otherworldly.

Dori knew she needed one of the hairs, but she didn't want to hurt the horse. He turned his head, whinnying at her, as if to say it was alright. Dori looked over at Rune, who was balancing on the balls of his feet, ready to jump if need be. A small nod from him and Dori focused back on the horse.

"Sorry, friend, if this hurts. I just need one. We need it to save someone important." Dori braced herself before using her fingers to separate out one singular hair from his mane. She followed the length of the hair up to where it was attached to the horse, grasped as tight as she could, sent one last silent prayer to anyone listening, and pulled.

Chapter 20

The feral screech echoed throughout the sky. Dori snatched her hand back from the stallion, his hair firmly grasped in her palm, for an instant thinking that's where the noise came from. The screeched sounded again and that's when she saw the shadow of wings moving swiftly across the ground. Instantly Rune, Callan, and Gunner went on the defense, positioning themselves around Dori.

  Gunner pulled a piece of string out of his pocket, using it to pull his hair up and out of his face. He reached into the other pocket of his jacket, pulling out a pair of sparring gloves, and tossed his jacket to the side, before slipping the gloves onto his hands. Rune reached into his bag, pulling out two old fashioned looking handguns. He had told her the day they met that he was bringing protection with him. Rune whistled at Gunner and then tossed him one of the guns, which Gunner caught easily. Callan was busy digging through his own small bag, quickly pulling out two smaller daggers, one for each hand.

The three men positioned themselves to make sure they had the maximum coverage over Dori.

Three very large monkey soldiers hit the ground in front of them, dressed in armor and looking every bit as intimidating as the one in Rune's house.

"We've been looking for you," the one in the middle spat out, his wings flaring out as he grunted at them.

"Found us," Rune gritted out between his teeth. His body was tense with anticipation, ready for a fight. Callan and Gunner shifted the same way, their bodies finally full of the magic and strength that had been denied to them for ten years.

"Give us the girl and maybe we'll spare you," another soldier yelled at them.

"Not gonna happen." Callan moved an inch closer to Dori as he spoke, leaving no doubt that the only way through this was to fight. Before anyone else could move another screech echoed through the sky and the sound of multiple pairs of wings could be heard flapping above them, making it clear to Dori and her warriors that they were vastly outnumbered.

Rune was the one that set fire to the situation, by turning around quickly and getting two shots off into the sky. Mere seconds later two giant bodies fell from the sky, dead, with bullet holes right between the eyes. A breath later and all hell broke loose. The three soldiers in front of them went on the attack while soldiers from the sky started swooping down towards them.

Rune and Gunner took turns shooting into the sky, Rune taking out more than Gunner, while Callan kept the three on the ground busy with his daggers. Dancing around them, weaving and dodging when hits were coming his way, and then slicing and stabbing as he moved around. One of the soldiers managed to knock one of Callan's daggers out of his hands, and for that Callan pulled back and socked him right in the jaw, knocking him out cold.

Shot after shot coming from Rune and Gunner, evening out their odds a bit, but soon the bullets ran out. After his last bullet Gunner waited until one of the soldiers flew close enough to the ground that he was in reach, and then he grabbed the soldier's wings, threw him to the ground, and continually stomped on him and threw punches at him until he was knocked out.

Dori, not knowing where to give her attention, heard a screech and turned to see two soldiers flying towards her with their arms out, as if they were prepared to grab hold of her and take her away. Dori screamed, turned, and started running.

It took only seconds before she felt the hands of the two soldiers clamp on to her arms and start to lift her up. Kicking her feet, Dori was trying everything she could to get them to let her go, but nothing was working. Panic started filling every inch of her body, if they took her to the Enchantress the fight was over.

Rune turned and, after seeing Dori's feet start to rise from the ground, ran towards her while taking his hands and reaching in the back of his waist band, pulling out his own two daggers. Instantly he stopped and whipped both daggers towards the soldiers pulling Dori away. The moment the daggers left his hands Rune started running towards her again.

The first dagger hit its mark, the very top of the spine on one of the soldiers, causing that soldier to drop Dori's arm and hit the ground, dead. The second dagger hit the hand that was still holding onto Dori. In reaction to the pain, the soldier dropped Dori and before he knew what had happened Rune jumped, using a fallen soldier as a jumping off point, and launched himself at the injured soldier. They collided in the air and Rune used his momentum to pull the soldier to the ground with him.

Where Rune pulled a third dagger from, Dori wasn't sure. But there he stood, over top of the soldier, holding a dagger to his throat.

"No one touches her," growled, and with that Rune sliced the dagger across his throat. The soldier was dead less than a minute later. Dori could feel the bile rising in her throat at the sight of so much blood. Rune turned to her with a feral look in his eyes. He walked up to her, using the back of his hand to gently brush the hair out of her eyes, and then in the blink of an eye he was behind her, launching his fist into another soldier's face. The fight was still going on.

Dori turned around and saw just how far the fight had gone. There were soldier bodies littering the ground. Two soldiers were left. Gunner and Callan were trading punch for punch with them. Rune walked up behind them without being detected, and on the first soldier Rune grabbed his head and quickly snapped his neck. The last soldier took a few steps back, realizing that he was now the one outnumbered.

Callan went to step forward, prepared to end the soldier's life, when Rune held a hand up to stop him. The soldier looked at Rune, confused.

"Go. Tell the Enchantress what happened here. Tell her no one touches Dori. Tell her we're coming for her. Her days are numbered."

The soldier didn't waste any time, as he turned and flew off into the sky.

Chapter 21

Later that night, sitting around a small campfire for warmth, Dori couldn't get something out of her mind. Staring at the dancing flames as they rose up into the night, she was turning one thought over and over in her head. Rune sat across the flames from her, watching her closely, not saying a word. Callan and Gunner were congratulating each other on their successes of the day, not concerned with how quiet their companions had become.

"Ask it." His low voice carried over the dancing fire, startling Dori out of her own thoughts. Her eyes lifted up, zeroing in on his and finding it almost impossible to shift her eyes away from his. Dori took a few deep breaths, figuring out the best way to ask it.

"What happened to make the Enchantress who she is?"

If Rune showed surprise at the direction of her question, he didn't show it. It hadn't been the thought festering in her mind when he first spoke. That question Dori didn't know if she had it in her to ask, at least not yet. At her question both Callan and Gunner stopped their conversation.

"We don't fully know. When she came to us, she had enchanted herself to appear a certain way. She looked friendly and kind, just lost and in need of help. It wasn't until it was too late that we saw her for what she really was. A nasty, green-skinned witch who had no problem using dark forces to gain power over the land and its people," Callan answered.

"Wait, why is her skin tinted green?" Dori looked over to him.

"When a person abuses power, when they let evil into their hearts and embrace it as the Enchantress has done, it turns into a sickness. It seeps into every pore, every vein, every fibre of their being. The magic is what's keeping her body alive at this point. The evil she's taken in is acting like an infection under her skin and it creates a green tint. It's something that we know to keep a look out for. The only reason she got past us was because of the enchantment she cast on herself. Without that, we would have known what she was straight away, and we would have done away with her before she was able to strip our power from us. As far as we can tell, Briella isn't far from that. She'll be going down that same path soon, if she hasn't already."

The crackle of the embers filled the air as Dori started to get a clearer picture of who the Enchantress was. Only someone with an already tainted heart would embrace that type of magic. There would be no redemption for her, there would be no mercy when they fought the Enchantress. It would be her or them.

"Are all witches in your world bad?" Dori inquired.

"No, not all. You've met Elowynn, she's a good witch. There are more out there, somewhere. Some witches are more powerful than others, those are the ones we usually hear about. But there are lesser witches who go through their day to day lives without anyone knowing what they truly are."

"Why doesn't Elowynn take out her sisters. Fight Briella, fight the Enchantress?" It was something that Dori had been wondering since the night of dancing lights. Rune spoke up this time, unwilling to stay quiet any longer.

"The little that I've gotten from talking to her, Elowynn and her two sisters had a strained relationship as kids. The Enchantress and Elowynn disagreed on almost everything. The Enchantress viewed power as something to obtain to rule, while Elowynn always viewed it as a tool to help, nothing more. Briella usually sided with the Enchantress, and Elowynn was cast to the side for trying to do what was right. The moment she was able Elowynn left them behind for a better life. Once the Enchantress took over Oz, Elowynn had some tough decisions to make.

Elowynn and the Enchantress have different priorities. Those priorities affect the way their magic works. The Enchantress has only one goal, to gain as much power as she can so that she can rule the entire land. No one really knows what she wants to rule for, but knowing what she's capable of, we know it wouldn't be safe for anyone. That makes her magic toxic.

Elowynn has always prioritized who she calls her people. The people of the forest. Elowynn will do anything for their safety. It's why households of citizens flocked to the forest when the Enchantress took power. Elowynn's magic is tied to that forest, and only as long as she's alive and well will that forest protect them.

If the Enchantress was able to kill Elowynn it would leave dozens of families unprotected, and the Enchantress would swoop in and slaughter them all. Elowynn's magic is steeped in protection. While it still is very strong, she would never fully put her people at risk, and because of that the Enchantress would be able to defeat her in the end." Rune explained.

Dori listened to every word Rune spoke, understanding more why they weren't attacked until they were out in the open. The forest they were in had been doing what it could to keep them safe until they weren't under the protection of its canopy. With everything that she had learned, there was only one question left on her mind.

"How do you kill a witch as strong as the Enchantress?" Dori asked, knowing that without the Enchantress, Briella wouldn't stand a chance against the guardians.

All three men looked at her, but it was Gunner that answered.

"Cut off her fucking head."

The other two just grunted in agreement.

Chapter 22

The four travelers spent the next two days traveling towards the Emerald City. It wouldn't have taken so long if they hadn't had to ensure they weren't seen by any of the Enchantresses spies.

Dori had never walked so much in her entire life. There was something calming about walking through the forests, breathing in the fresh air. The three friends had fallen back into old ways, constantly ribbing each other and trading stories back and forth about days that were long ago.

Dori was having a hard time keeping her eyes off of Rune, watching how different he was now that his curse was broken. Still a surly, gruff man at times, Rune had surprised her with how much he actually smiled and laughed. He would check in with her constantly, not always verbally, but with a glance and an eyebrow raise.

Dori found herself walking side by side with Rune most often, usually in silence, as everything they wanted to say to each other needed to be said in very different circumstances. It had been days since he kissed her, and still she could feel the touch of his lips on hers, the way his hands cradled her face and the way his scent lingered in her nose. Walking beside him but not being able to touch him was a strange kind of torture. The pull between the two of them was still there. He was ridiculously attractive to her before, and now that he smiled and had light in his eyes, it almost hurt her to look at him. A guardian warrior of a land far from her own, they would have nothing in common. And yet, occasionally, Dori found herself wondering 'what if'?

At night she would lay down beside him, with the fire on the other side of her to keep her warm, but nothing untoward would happen. As they slept their bodies, like magnets, would pull towards each other, and when Dori woke in the mornings Rune's strong arms were always wound around her, keeping her warm and safe until the sun rays lit up the sky.

Her time in this land wouldn't go on forever, those quiet moments with Rune felt like a gift, the memories something she would never give up. If she couldn't keep him forever, at least she would be able to remember the few nights where she was able to sleep underneath a starry sky wrapped in arms of a man that ripped warriors out of the sky to protect her.

On the last day of their travels through the woods they were traveling along the outside wall of the city. The Enchantress had been in charge for a decade, and in that time, she spent very little energy on fixing up any of the city's infrastructure. The wall around the city was in desperate need of fixing, along with the roads and buildings throughout. They took a vote, and everyone agreed that marching through the city would be the quickest way to be caught by the Enchantress's guard. There were a few holes in the wall closer to the castle that they could slip through.

At last, just after lunch, they managed to find a hole in the wall and all four of them squeezed through the wall, looking around for the Enchantress's guard, but like most of the city, the castle grounds appeared to be vacant. This used to be a place of community and coming together. Markets would be held just outside the castle doors, and everyone was welcome. Looking around at the empty space, the dead grass and lack of life, Rune's heart ached at what had been caused by their failure.

Cautiously walking up to the front gate, Dori looked around at all the plant pots and flower beds with nothing but dead plants and leaves filling them. No one had given any love to this place in a long time. Putting her hand on the castle wall, Dori swore she could feel it's sorrow, as if the castle itself was sentient and hurting. Callan walked up behind her, putting a hand on her shoulder. Dori could see in his eyes the pain he was trying to hold back. Gunner almost looked like he was going to be sick, as he picked up a plant pot that had been tipped over and partially broken.

The three guardians looked around in horror at the home that they had been raised in, disgusted at how much of it had been left in disrepair. Rune took the lead, opening the door and entering first, not knowing what waited any of them inside, but ready for the entire nightmare to be over.

While the outside of the castle hadn't changed much (other than becoming vacant with a few bricks here and there that were crumbling) that wasn't the case on the inside. As the thick wooden door squeaked open it became apparent just how bad things had gotten.

Rune took the lead, stepping into the castle. The thick air staggered his breath. All around him there were thick nasty looking vines covered in thorns. Crawling up the walls, on the ceiling, covering the floors. The stench that they gave off was that of a rotting compost pile, Dori had to fight the urge to cover her nose, knowing it wouldn't help keep the stench away.

From the foyer there were three different hallways to choose from, and one staircase. One of the hallways looked completely overtaken by the insidious plant. The vines had wound their way up the banister of the staircase, leaving very little space for anyone to go up or down the stairs themselves.

"We have three choices, I guess." Looking around, every path felt ominous to Gunner.

"South will be in the throne room, which is up the stairs and down the hall. The Enchantress won't be far from him. That's where we'll be going." Rune's gruff voice, aimed at Dori, vibrated off the walls.

"Which leaves us with a choice. Which hall of nightmares do we risk going down?" It had been agreed upon that Callan and Gunner would hunt down the broom ashes.

"Do either look ideal? There are a set of bedrooms down the hall to the left, I could see that being where the sister is lodged. If she's smart, she'll have hidden her broom somewhere else in the castle, the dungeons even. But I have a feeling these sisters aren't as clever as they think."

"You don't think they know about how to break the curse?" Dori asked Callan.

"I think they don't believe we'd find out how to do it. The ego on them will tell them their brooms are safe in their rooms," Callan explained, and Gunner nodded in agreement.

"It's settled, then. That's the way we go." Callan looked over at Dori. She had changed everything for them. Became the friend he didn't know he needed. Callan knew they had to split up. That meant sending his friend possibly to her death. Callan loved her protectively, like a brother would, but he had absolute trust in Rune to defend her to the end.

Making eye contact with Rune, Callan could see the fierceness he felt towards Dori. Whether Rune meant to or not, he had fallen hard and fast. It was one of the things Callan had appreciated about his guardian brother. When he loved, he loved deeply, and may the gods help anyone who tried take that away from him.

"Dori." Callan reached over to her, enveloping her in a hug that said everything he couldn't.

"I'll see you again, Callan. This isn't the end. This is the beginning." Dori pulled away, looking her friend in the eyes. The goofy and kind stranger turned family. For him, for all of them, she would walk into that throne room. She would walk in, but if she was being honest with herself, she knew she wouldn't be walking out. Rune grasped Callan's hand and pulled him into a hug.

"Take care of her."

Rune merely grunted and nodded his head as he pulled away. Quickly glancing at Dori Rune looked back, pulling Callan close.

"Take care of yourselves. If things take a turn, get out. Get out while you can before they can do this again." Rune was looking past Callan to Gunner, who was embracing Dori. Callan and Rune shared a look. Gunner had been put through, arguably, the most. At least within the three of them. No one knew just yet how involved the curse was at messing South up. But Gunner, anyone could see it on his face. The way he carried himself. How he flinched far too easily at loud noises still, and how he was always walking behind everyone else, not to protect them, but to be protected by them.

The curse may have been broken for him, but the memories remained. Gunner had a lot to work through and a lot to forget. While still looking at Gunner, Rune leaned over to Callan and whispered.

"If it looks like things are going wrong, get him out. Don't hesitate."

Callan didn't even bother arguing, he just nodded. Both men knew they would move the planets and the stars to keep anything more from damaging their traumatized friend.

Dori pulled away from Gunner and looked at the men as a group.

"Well, what do you say? Let's knock these bitches down off their pedestals. Let's go get your King back."

Rune knew then that he loved her. The woman who fell from the sky and turned his world on its head. The woman that stood up for his brother when she didn't have a clue about where she was or the danger she was in. The woman who walked through minds, awakened hearts, and inspired courage. He loved her with every breath in his body.

Just then a cackling echoed off the walls and the vines that surrounded them on every surface started moving around.

"Well, there goes our element of surprise. Dori, run."

With that Rune took her hand and hauled her up the stairs, without looking back at his brothers.

Callan and Gunner took off running down the hall, jumping over the vines that had started moving towards them. Callan started swinging his dagger out at any vine that got within reach. Gunner followed behind him, keeping an eye out for anything trying to pop out at them.

Chapter 23

After what felt like ages, going around hallway to hallway, fighting against the vines, Gunner and Callan finally found the hidden door. While the vines took it upon themselves to grow up the walls, and even on the roof, this was the only door in the entire hallway that the vines seemed to be avoiding. There was no way to tell if Briella was in there until they opened the door. On the outside, the door looked as normal as every other door in the castle. It was wooden, adorned with black metal fixings and a black metal handle.

Callan lifted his booted foot up and slammed it into the door. The wooden door smashed open, cracking against the wall as it hit. The room itself was simple. A small bed against one wall with a thin looking blanket on top of it and a thin pillow. On the other end of the room was a small table that held a washing basin and a cloth. There was also a small dressing cabinet with double doors, both of which were closed. The broom wasn't visible, nor was its owner; the room itself seemed to echo with quietness.

Gunner went to take a step over the threshold, but Callan grabbed him and pulled him back, shaking his head back and forth. Gunner instantly looked into the room to find whatever the danger was that Callan saw and came up empty.

"What …"

Callan held a finger up to his mouth to shush Gunner. Callan may not have seen the witch, but the air inside the room felt off. Magic sometimes left a small residue behind. Sometimes it was a smell, sometimes it was a sound. In this moment, the air Callan could feel from the doorway felt as though it was vibrating wrong. Not all was as it seemed in the witch's room. Turning to Gunner, Callan whispered.

"We can't take things as they first appear. A simple concealing spell could have her right in front of our eyes, and we wouldn't even know it." It all seemed to be very convenient. The only thing that would have made him more suspicious was if the broom in question was laying on the bed. Both men observed the room for another moment, trying to see past what magic was hiding. A voice echoed through the room from a hidden source.

"Very clever."

Feminine, and cruel, Callan could picture the calculated smile on the witch's face. Callan sneered.

"Briella. I thought that was you, hiding behind your magic like the coward you are. Are you going to show yourself, now that the gig is up?" Still refusing to step into the room, Callan made sure that one hand was holding the handle of a dagger that was still sheathed, just in case.

"Where would the fun be in that? Come in and find me boys." Her voice seemed to sweep around the room as if carried by the wind. "That is, unless you're scared … Gunner." Gunner's initial reaction was to snarl at her and storm directly into the room for the reference to the curse that they had placed on him. Thankfully, Callan had a good head on his shoulders. He could tell it was a trap and pulled Gunner back, once again, shaking his head.

"It's not going to be as easy, this time. We won't be unknowingly walking into a trap. You want to beat us; you're actually going to have to fight us this time." Callan pulled himself out of the doorway and into the hallway. Close enough to still hear Briella, but out of her sight so she couldn't see what he was doing. There was a small cloth bag hanging off his belt, barely the size of a dinner roll. Callan pulled it off his belt, opened the tie, and slowly dumped a small amount of red powder into the palm of his hand. Gunner saw what he was doing and, when Callan was ready, Gunner backed up out of the doorway as Callan jumped in front of the door, blowing the powder into the room.

As the dust settled Callan started muttering an incantation under his breath, and within three heartbeats a silhouette started to become visible, sitting on the bed. Briella, with her mud brown hair and face set in a snarl, was watching Callan with confusion. Her over confidence in her own magic made her believe that she was the most powerful witch in the room.

What she didn't realize was that, while their fathers ensured the three boys were well trained in battle and combat, it was their mothers that would spend evening after evening teaching them all they needed to know about magic, the elements, and the nature that surrounded them. Callan easily broke the enchantment Briella had cast to keep herself hidden. Both men scowled at Briella, ready to end her and her sister's reign.

Briella, realizing that they could see her, jumped off the bed and held herself in a defensive position. Callan and Gunner glanced at each other before silently agreeing to a plan. Gunner shouted and charged Briella, who in a panic at the last moment put up a protective shield around herself. Gunner stopped just short of the shield and barred his teeth at her in utter frustration. Puffing her own chest up, an obviously fake act of confidence, Briella spat at him.

"You'll never defeat us. You can't break South's curse. He's ours for as long as we want him, and my sister isn't giving him up for anything." Her snide comments were a pitiful attempt to distract them while she figured out another way to get them out of her room. Briella was surprised at how much power they seemed to have gained back. Callan saw no need to engage her in any kind of conversation, so he started looting the room while ignoring her. He started with her bed, flipping it over in one motion, looking for the broom.

Gunner, however, was ripe for confrontation, and as long as she was trapped in the corner of her room, in a trap she made for herself, he was going to play.

"Your sister is an idiot. She must be, she left you here all by yourself, defenseless." Standing there, staring her down, Gunner so badly wanted that shield to falter, even for a quick second. It would be all he needed to tear her throat out.

"I'm not defenseless." A slight tremor in her voice gave away the nerves she was trying to hide. Callan glanced back over at her.

"You're hiding behind a spell in the corner of a room while two full powered guardians tear it apart. How are you not defenseless?"

"I can leave whenever I want. I can. And once my sister finds out how you've destroyed my room and how you've attacked me, she's going to peel the skin from your body." The last word faded quickly as Callan walked straight up to Briella, towering over her by a few feet. His eyes were dark with rage at the memories of what her and her sister had put him and his friends through. Gunner stood silently beside him.

"Let it be known that it was your sister, not you, that managed to defeat us last time. You are no mastermind. You're just her family pet." Callan spat back at her, the spit hitting the shield before sliding down it.

"Your sister isn't going to last the hour, let alone another day, in power. You may have gotten the drop on us before, but we're mostly put back together now. And guess what, we're pissed. She wants to take the skin from our bones? I want to do worse to her, and if I get my way, I'll be doing worse to you, as well. Enjoy the safety of that bubble, bitch. It won't last for long." Callan backed away from her and, once again, started speaking in low tones as he poured more red dust into his palm. As his words finished, he blew the powder at her and the shield she put around herself started to falter.

"What ... what is that stuff?" Briella tried backing further into the wall, no longer able to hide the concern written across her face.

"Poppy dust. Very powerful." Briella's eyes widened in horror before she started conjuring energy balls into her hands, throwing them at Callan and Gunner the moment her shield had completely failed. Gunner jumped out of the way as one headed straight for him, letting it instead hit the clothing cupboard, destroying it in one blast.

Looking over at its remnants on the floor, Callan smiled. There, sitting amongst the broken pieces of wood, was Briella's broom. Gunner looked at it, and then back at Briella, who to her credit, started understanding what they really were looking for. She opened her palm and her broom shot straight into her hand. Callan pulled two daggers out of the waistband of his pants and growled at Briella.

"We're getting that broom, one way or another." And before she could register which way the threat was coming, both guardians charged at her. Many things could be said for Briella, but one thing was certain. She knew when she was beaten. Throwing the broom to one side of the room, Briella bolted the other way and, when both guardians lunged for the broom, she headed for the door, ran down the hallway, and out of sight.

"I'm sure we don't have long before Briella finds the Enchantress and lets her know what we're up to here. We have to hurry!" Gunner grabbed the broom while Callan looked out into the hallway to make sure the coast was clear. They had the broom, but they needed to find a way to burn it in a flame hot enough to cause ashes almost immediately.

Callan had one more item left in his arsenal of magic. A small pouch of dust that, when poured on top of a fire, caused the flames to burn as hot as the sun in the sky. It wouldn't last long, but hopefully long enough for at least part of the broom to burn. Gunner pulled the splintered pieces of the cupboard together as Callan used a small ball of his own energy to light it on fire.

"Alright, here we go!" Callan opened the small bag with the magical mix and poured it on top of the open flame. Almost instantly the fire roared up to twice its size and the heat coming from it was almost unbearable. Gunner held the broom up, trying to decide which end to stick into the fire, and ultimately decided the straw on the end would burn fastest. He placed the broom, straw end first, into the fire and watched it catch. Gunner left it in there for a moment, before pulling the broom out. Flames danced on the straw and started climbing up the handle. Waiting until he saw it wasn't going to go out, Gunner put the broom down on the floor as they both stood back and watched.

Only a moment later the burnt straw started turning black, little pieces of it breaking off, leaving little piles of ash on the floor. Gunner pulled out the small spell jar from his pocket. Inside the melted snow, now water, sloshed around the hair from a horse of a different color. He popped the cork open, careful not to spill anything.

Callan very carefully pulled the rest of the burning broom away from the small piles of ash. Callan then bent down and, holding the small bag from the earlier magic dust, pushed as much ash into the bag as he could manage. He then stood up, walked over to Gunner and, as Gunner held the spell jar open, Callan poured what ash he could into the jar.

Once the ash hit the snowy water the mixture started stirring itself, creating a small vortex. Gunner immediately put the cork back in the bottle. The last step would be to say the spell the Dori held in her pocket. Both men took a mere second of thought before they ran out the door, and back down the hallway they came from.

Chapter 24

Rune led Dori down a long empty corridor. The vines had made their way to this level, and while they were moving, they seemed to be moving out of Rune and Dori's way, as if they were corralling them to a certain spot. The doors to the throne room were propped open, giving Rune a sick feeling in his stomach.

"Whatever happens in that room, I'm glad I came here," Dori whispered to Rune as they shuffled down the hallway. Rune stopped for a moment and pulled her close, leaning his forehead on hers and maintaining eye contact.

"Whatever happens in that room, meeting you healed bits of me I didn't know needed healing. I'm glad you came here too."

Rune gave her a sweet kiss before they both turned and, walking hand in hand, stepped into the throne room.

The room was a large rectangle, with mostly empty space and multiple large windows. The large windows lining one wall were covered with bulky curtains and the floor looked covered in mud and muck. At the other end of the room stood the

Enchantress, watching them and assessing every move they made. Standing in front of her was a line of ten of her royal guards, all holding spears and shields, as if they expected trouble. The only thing stopping Rune from charging straight at her was the person sitting on the throne.

It had been a long time since Rune had seen his friend. Time, and the curse, had done nothing but suck the life out of him. His skin had lost all color and had started turning grey. His once beautiful eyes were bloodshot and sunken in. The clothes he was wearing were stained, threads were coming loose, and the clothes themselves were almost starting to fall off him due to the weight that he must have lost. Rune almost vomited seeing how bad things had gotten for South. And there, lounging on South with her arm wrapped around his shoulders from behind, was the Enchantress.

There she stood, in her black silk gown, mesh black sleeves reaching her wrists. Her long silky hair pulled up into a high ponytail, with what looked like priceless jewelry adorning her neck and wrists. There she stood, green skin and all, wearing South's crown with a malicious grin on her face.

"North, how good of you to visit. My men have been looking for you," the Enchantresses voice purred at him.

"You know by now that some of them were competent enough to find me. Not that they were competent enough to defeat me, of course," Rune grunted back at her. Dori was having a hard time keeping her breathing under control. It felt like she was standing outside right before a tornado was going to hit. The air held a tense vibration, Dori was afraid to make any sudden movements.

"Oh, and one other thing. The name is Rune." That was the first thing he said that seemed to have any effect on the Enchantress. She stuttered for a small moment and the cat like grin lowly disappeared from her face.

"Oh look, your little friend helped you find your name." She sneered with disgust.

Dori could feel the exact moment the Enchantress turned to her. Chills went from the tip of her head straight down to her toes. Doing her best to keep her head held high, Dori refused to look away.

"Not just me. Callan and Gunner say, well they say, 'burn in hell!'" The pride in Rune's voice towards Dori and everything she had already helped with was blatant. The grip the Enchantress had on South's shoulders started to tighten as she was having issues reigning in her anger.

"Only took you ten years. Tell me, however did you louts learn how to break the curses? Did my foul earth loving sister have anything to do with it?" The Enchantress questioned.

"She gave us the clues, but the big win goes to Dori, here. Without her it never would have happened. She was the key we needed, and as a gift to her we're going to knock you off that throne and serve her your head on a pike." Rune took a step forward, causing the Enchantresses soldiers to respond with five steps forward before she raised a hand, and they stopped in their tracks.

"Say what you want, but I'm the one up here with the power, while you're standing down there, no army in sight." The Enchantress stood tall with a smug look across her face. Dori could feel Rune's hand in hers tightening the angrier he became.

"This wasn't your power to take. This wasn't your kingdom to have!" Rune's voice echoed off the throne room walls.

"I wanted it, so I took it, and what makes you more angry, Rune? The fact that you couldn't stop it or the fact that you weren't able to get your buddy out and he had to live with me all of this time?" While speaking, the Enchantress took the opportunity to run her hands through South's hair and then caress his cheek and South didn't have the energy to do anything but sit there and let her. Rune had seen enough as he let his anger guide him. He let go of Dori's hand and jumped headfirst into the guards, tossing them around like pillows. It looked like he was making progress, until they ended up circling him. Guards started getting punches in and if they kept this up Rune wouldn't be able to break free. Dori had to do something.

"Rune, she's trying to distract you! Remember why we're here! Remember South!" Dori was shouting, trying to get Rune's attention. The Enchantress's hand flew out and threw Dori into the wall, her body crumpling down once she made contact.

"Dori!" Rune snapped as he saw her limp body lying on the ground. He reached around and grabbed the sword from the guard in front of him, head butting the guard and dropping him. Rune then aggressively started grabbing any soldier that got in his way, running them through with the sword. But the Enchantress wasn't going stop coming for him.

"Aww, is that concern in your voice? Do you think you have love in your heart for the stranger from another land? You know how that's going to go, don't you?" The Enchantress kept pulling his attention two separate ways. South was on the other end of the room from Dori. Every time Rune looked over at South the Enchantress would fuss over him like a lover. Dori started letting out small whimpers of pain, pulling Rune's eyes back to her on the other side of the room.

"Shut up!" he shouted at the Enchantress as he started marching back over to Dori's body.

"She won't stay here with you. Not forever. She'll be pulled back home, worlds away from here, and you won't be able to go." The Enchantress taunted Rune with his worst nightmare.

Just as Rune reached her, Dori's unconscious body started rising from the floor and floating towards the Enchantress, who had a handout, using her magic to pull Dori in. Dori's body was lowered on the right side of the Enchantress while South still sat on her left side.

"I said shut up you witch!" Rune bellowed out at her.

"Back down now and maybe I'll be lenient. I won't take her head from her body and use it as my own. Maybe I'll leave her unharmed. Unharmed, and in the arms of my cousins. You remember them, don't you? They seemed to have taken a liking to her when they first met her. I'm sure they have a few things they would like to get off their chests."

Rune knew better, and yet he struck first. He charged at her. The Enchantress started chanting, creating an energy ball to throw at Rune, but Rune picked up a shield from the dead guards and used it to deflect the Enchantresses attack. Rune was able to deflect two more before the shield was so badly damaged, it was worthless. Rune tossed it straight at the Enchantress, which she deflected with her magic.

"You shut your filthy mouth about her. Your cousins weren't worth the dirt on the bottom of her shoes. If they ever come anywhere near her again, they'll have to deal with me, and I haven't been in the best of moods as of late." Spit flew out of his mouth as he tried to distract the Enchantress with is words. However, it wasn't him that succeeded in distracting her, it was his people.

Outside a rallying war cry rose up, loud enough that it could be clearly heard in the throne room, pulling everyone's attention. Citizens from the forest could be heard flooding the streets of the city in protest of what had happened to their land.

"What is that racket?" the Enchantress asked, genuinely looking confused for a moment, and Rune shot a feral grin her way.

"My people. Our people. They are done with you. They're fighting back!" Hearing his people fight for what was right, fight to regain control of their land, refilled Rune with energy and passion. Before she was able to respond Rune lunged closer and it was enough for him to reach her. He grabbed her around the throat with his bare hands, bare hands that had small cuts and dirt smudged on them. He started squeezing, looking her dead in the eyes.

"You picked the wrong farm girl. You picked the wrong friend. You picked the wrong throne. You picked the wrong people. You picked wrong, and now I'm going to make you pay for it." Rune growled, his hot breath covering her face as he let his rage take over.

The anger coursing through Rune started ringing in his ears. He could see the life exiting her body. Her eyes were starting to bulge, and her hands were trying to claw at his.

On the ground Dori started coming to, and the first thing she saw was something Rune hadn't noticed.

"Rune, watch out!" Dori managed to get out while holding her side and sliding her body up the way. The warning came too late as Briella appeared and launched a magical pulse at him. Unprotected and unprepared, the pulse knocked him away from the Enchantress, who fell to the ground, grabbing at her throat and gulping down the air as if it was the only thing to quench her thirst.

Briella didn't stop there. Pulse after pulse she shot towards Rune's chest, not giving him a second of reprieve. Dori was too weak to do anything but watch Rune be attacked as he yelled out in pain. Only when Briella was standing beside her sister did she pull back as the Enchantress slowly stood up again.

"Thank you, sister. You're timing has never been more perfect." The Enchantress dusted her clothing off, smirking at the monster her sister had evolved in to. She walked up and spat on Rune.

"The other two are in the castle somewhere. They overpowered me in my room, but I managed to get away. I knew if I found you, we could defeat them together." Briella was trying to keep her sister's attention, but more rallying cries came from outside following by the sounds of swords hitting shields and guns going off.

"Keep an eye on them, Briella, I want to make sure our outside forces are holding strong." The Enchantress moved to the window, turning her own back on the room, wanting to ensure that her guards were still keeping the rebels out of the castle. Having a hard time seeing anything she raised her arms in the air, chanting as a murder of crows started circling just outside of the window. With cloudy eyes she stood there in a trance, getting an update from a bird's eye view.

Rune, lying on the floor, took stock of what was going on. It all seemed a bit familiar. South was out of commission. Callan and Gunner were working hard on breaking the curse, but they were running out of time.

"Seems history is repeating itself, isn't it Rune? The last time we had you in this position things didn't work so well for you, did it?" With the flick of Briella's wrist Rune went flying against the wall, knocking the air out of his chest. Tears stung his eyes as he allowed himself, just for a moment, to consider what would happen if they lost again.

"Only this time we won't make the same mistake. Leaving you three alive last time was a small mercy. But don't worry, it won't happen again."

Briella held her hand level as a bright ball of electricity and light started to grow. Her wild eyes were fixed on him, and he was helpless to do anything about it. Rune had lost his confidence in the situation, just for a small moment, he allowed himself to imagine his land and people if the guardians lost this battle. That was enough to affect the strength of his magic, and because of it he was having a hard time throwing off Briella's magic.

"Like I said, history is repeating itself. Say hello to your friends on the other side of the rainbow." Briella chirped at him as she prepared to end his life. As Briella reared her arm back to send the pulse his way, a dagger was shoved through her heart from the back.

"That's not necessary. I'm right here, bitch." Dori twisted the dagger in Briella's back before using all of her strength to pull it out. Briella fell to the ground, gasping for breath. Dori stood over her, like an avenging angel.

Rune slid to the ground, but his eyes were stuck on his Dori. The sun was shining in through the window behind her, giving her an almost ethereal appearance. Blood was dripping from the dagger and, as Briella was gasping for breath, Rune slowly stood, reaching to take the dagger from Dori, the same dagger that he had given her after he saw her defending Gunner when they were attacked by the mob. The same dagger that he told her to protect herself with. She had saved his life with it. Dori handed it over without a second thought and Rune slowly stood up and stood over Briella, who's eyes were wide with disbelief.

"You have no power here, Briella. Not anymore." And with that Rune stabbed the dagger into her heart. The Enchantresses came back into her body just in time to see Rune kill her sister. She let out a horrific scream of anger and pain.

Rune and Dori stood watching her, side by side, breathing heavy. There was no time to rest, as the Enchantress started heading their way, intent on making them pay. Dori and Rune stood taller, bracing themselves, as they still had unfinished business; they still had a friend to save.

Chapter 25

Callan and Gunner ran into the throne room as the Enchantress shrieked at the sight of Briella's body. They quickly ran straight over to Dori, thrusting the small spell jar into her hands.

"Here. Go!" Gunner didn't have to say much, as he took up a fighting stance facing the Enchantress. Dori, somewhat still shaken from what she did to Briella, patted her pocked for the vial from Elowynn. Rune placed his hand on her shoulder briefly.

"Hurry! I'll keep her occupied. Callan, Gunner, stand back just in case. If she gets past me, I'll need you both to get Dori out of here," Rune stated as he turned to focus on the Enchantress.

Dori tore the cork out of the small glass tube and dumped a piece of parchment into her hand. Quickly unrolling it she turned it around in her hand once, and then again.

Emohek ilecal pon sereht

The words made no sense to her, but she would have to trust in Elowynn. The doors on both sides of the room burst open as more guards started pouring in, eyes glowing green from being spelled by the Enchantress. Callan and Gunner immediately started fighting, keeping the guards away from Dori.

Dori was out of time. She threw the vial holding the ingredients down to the floor, smashing it, as she started repeating the phrase, over and over,

"Emohek ilecal pon sereht. Emohek ilecal pon sereht," Dori repeated the phrase, and every time her voice became stronger and louder.

A wind started whipping through the room, causing the doors and windows to slam open. A loud ringing could be heard by Dori as the ground shook hard enough to knock everyone down. For the briefest of moments, after everyone fell, it was silent in the room, as the wind and noise all stopped. It didn't last long as the guardians and the guards all got back up and the fighting continued. Everyone was busy battling someone. So busy that no one noticed when the thumb on South's left hand started to move on its own.

The world was starting to come back to him. Bits and pieces started assaulting his brain as memories started filling in. The wind whipping around him was whispering his name ... *Roran ... Roran.* The name sounded so familiar. It brought him memories of four young boys pretending to sword fight with large sticks out in the orchard. Memories of a mother and father tending to his wounds and helping him strategize. Memories of markets full of life and community. The memory of his coronation, kneeling in front of his throne as his elderly father placed the crown atop of his head, passing on the responsibility of protecting their people, protecting Oz. *King Roran. It's time to rise.*

Slowly, piece by piece, he started to remember himself and the night the curse took over. Not fully aware how long he had been under the spell, Roran was aware he was the last to break out of it. All around him battles raged and there he sat, on the throne. No one had looked over at him yet. Callan and Gunner were fighting off guards who had caught up with them, and on the other end of things Rune and some strange woman were fighting off another set of guards. The Enchantress was standing over the dead body of her sister, attempting to call upon dark forces to bring her back from the dead.

Roran started flexing his fingers, the magic starting to trickle back in. He had to play his cards right. He would be far from battle ready, having been on the sidelines this entire time. His muscles and reflexes weren't what they once used to be, they felt weak and slow to respond. He would have to account for that, and his magic would take time coming back to him.

Pressing his toes into his boots he started rocking his heels back and forth, preparing to stand up. He didn't have to defeat everyone in the room, but he could become the distraction his friends needed to get the upper hand. Right when it looked like a soldier was about to get one over on Callan, Roran, King of Oz, took a deep breath and spoke.

"What the hell have you done to my kingdom?" His voice echoed off the walls and the Enchantress' face snapped up in shock, as did Rune's, Callan's, and Gunner's. Dori didn't know which way to look, still dizzy from performing the spell.

"No!" the Enchantress shouted out in disbelief, seeing the power she once held slipping out of her grasp.

"I want my kingdom back, witch." Roran slowly stood there, power circulating around his body, coming back to him faster than he expected. With each passing moment, each new breath, power grew within his veins. Rage seeped out of his eyes as he looked down on the woman that tried to take everything from him. His eyes and skin started healing in front of everyone, and the once ill guardian started looking more and more like the King this land needed.

The Enchantress could see the power radiating off of him. Everyone in the room took a step back as Roran started walking forward. A wind from seemingly nowhere started whipping around him, picking up dust, and creating a sphere of power. Water from the storm outside trickled through the windows and became caught up in the sphere. The fire from a lit torch jumped from its base and mixed itself into the sphere, all four elements surrounded King Roran.

The Enchantress was starting to feel desperate, quickly taking advantage of Rune staring in awe at his friend, she reached out and grabbed a weakened and distracted Rune by the back of the neck, placing the tip of her dagger at his jugular before anyone could stop her.

"You take one more step and he's done." She sneered.

Roran stopped moving but refused to back down completely.

"You aren't going to win here. You're already bleeding. Your army has abandoned you. You've lost." Roran spoke clearly, with the confidence of a King. True to his word, the power the Enchantress held over the guards in the room had faded and they fled the room in terror. The Enchantress became even more irate at the sight of it.

"My army was weak! I am not weak! I am strong! I have survived worse, I will survive this, I will survive you, Prince Roran!" Spit flew out of her mouth as the Enchantress raised her voice to Roran.

"Take the dagger away from his throat before I rip your own out for my pure amusement. And it's *King* Roran."

The Enchantress poked the dagger further into Rune's neck and a trickled of blood started to ooze out. Dori had to hold herself back from jumping in. Panic was setting into her bones. She couldn't see past the dagger at Rune's throat and her heart almost stopped when the blood dripped down. She couldn't hold herself back anymore.

"Please. Please stop. Let him go. You've done enough damage." Dori pleaded.

POPPY CURSES AND EMERALD SKIES

The Enchantress turned slightly to see Dori, but not enough to let Roran out of her sight.

"It's not enough. It will never be enough until I get what's rightfully mine, girl."

"But it's not yours. This land is not yours. If you were paying attention, you would have seen the signs. The land itself was telling you it did not belong to you. It dimmed its beauty around you and the animals all fled. The fields stopped producing harvest and the rain refused to fall. The land was telling you that you were not welcome. The people of this land ran to the forests for sanctuary and the trees hid them from your men. Everything was working against your reign of a land you say you deserve. How utterly stupid can you be?" Dori whispered the last part as if it were an afterthought.

The Enchantress jabbed Rune's neck again and he moaned out in pain.

"If you want to talk stupid, dearie, I would say trying to hurt the person holding your lover at knife point is more than stupid."

Dori shut her mouth there. The Enchantress turned her head back to Roran.

"You will let me walk away or your friend will die."

Roran didn't back down one inch. He stood confident in his choices, knowing Rune would understand every move he made.

"I don't think you were paying attention, so I'll say it one more time. Let him go. You can't win here."

Callan and Gunner remained stationary across the room, waiting for a moment when they could jump in. Gunner took a step forward, causing the Enchantress to look over at them and it gave Roran enough of a moment to raise his hand and shoot a sphere of dirt at her. If it hit Rune it would hurt, but it wouldn't do a lot of damage. However, it could be enough to knock her loose from Rune. But she turned in time to raise her other hand and deflect it.

"I warned you." With that she took her dagger and stabbed it into Rune's heart. Three things happened simultaneously.

One.

Roran took after his own name and bellowed out at the Enchantress, all the while one after another shooting spheres of fire, earth, water, and wind at her. Now that she was no longer holding Rune, who had fallen to the floor clutching the dagger hanging out of his chest, she was able to deflect and use her own magic to shoot pulses at Roran. Back and forth the went for each other, the deflected pulses and spheres were shattering stone on the walls where they were hitting.

Roran couldn't see anything but his rage. The rage that he felt for the woman that killed his best friend, his brother. The rage he felt at being held against his will by the bitch, for so long. The rage at the strife and suffering his people were caused at her hands. The rage at how his once beautiful land had been sucked dry by her arrogance and entitlement.

While Roran may have had the power to win this battle in the old days, he had been out of commission for so long. His powers had been dormant, and it took time to build up the kind of endurance he needed for this kind of battle and, physically, his body wasn't ready for it. While he kept his attacks up, he could feel in his core that, if it didn't end soon, it wouldn't end well. Still, the sight of Rune on the floor, dead, kept fueling the fire within him.

Two.

Callan and Gunner ran over to Rune, checking his pulse and looking him over.

"Rune!" Gunner looked the wound over while Callan made sure to block them from the two magical beings ripping the world apart. He muttered a small spell to bring up a shield. It wouldn't last past three blows of what they were throwing around, but it was better than nothing. Callan had to keep muttering the same words, over and over, or the shield would fall.

"Callan! He needs healing! His pulse is still there, but it's very weak! Callan!" Callan looked over at Gunner and nodded, acknowledging that he was listening, and when he did a rogue sphere hit his shield. He had two more before they would be back out in the open.

Gunner was scared to pull the dagger out. Every instinct from experience told him to leave it in, lest it create a bigger wound with a faster bleed. There was only so much he could do for Rune unless they got him to a healer immediately, and even then it would be touch and go.

"Roran! You need to end this!" But Roran was too far gone to hear Gunner's cries. There was nothing he could do but hold his friend and send out prayer after prayer to the spirits in the sky, asking for help.

Three.

Dori stood there, in utter horror, as Rune dropped to the ground. Roran and the Enchantress started exchanging blow after blow, but Dori couldn't move out of the way. She could barely breath. Every cell in her body was focused on Rune's face. On his closed eyes and partially opened mouth. On the dagger that was sticking out of his heart. His poor heart.

Amidst the battle, the shattering and cracking stone, the shouting that everyone else was doing, amidst all of it, Dori started hearing a familiar ringing in her ears. It was the same ringing that she had heard back in her small farmhouse. It seemed like ages ago that she was standing in her kitchen with a ringing in her ears every time she looked at the emerald that fell from the sky. The emerald was, once again, reaching out to communicate with her.

"*Dori…Dori…from over the rainbow you came, and now it's time.*" The emerald was still in her pocket and the moment it started speaking to her, Dori's hand naturally went in search of it. Grabbing it Dori was surprised at how cold it felt. It had been in her pocket nonstop since she woke up in this strange land. And yet it felt as if the emerald had just been pulled out of the freezer. The bite of cold on her hand was the only thing that jolted Dori's attention away from Rune.

As she pulled the emerald out of her pocket, slowly and with great confusion, Dori looked down at it. It was glowing as bright as the lights that danced in the sky. The bright shine of the green stone was illuminating the room. Callan and Gunner looked over in awe and shock as Dori held it in front of her own face, staring at it.

"Dori, forever destined to fall from the sky to save Oz. In this life, in every life, destined to be our savior. Standing against wickedness is why you came. Time to shine." The voice that spoke held a delicate tune, soothing and comforting.

The green light reflected off Roran, who had made his way across the room throughout his battle. The Enchantress also looked over and was dumbfounded.

"How the hell did you get that?" she screeched.

But Dori was beyond responding. If she was being honest, she didn't even hear the Enchantress talk to her. All she could hear was the emerald in her ears. The reflecting light on the emerald started moving around, giving the stone the illusion that it was dancing.

The Enchantress took the small moment that Roran was distracted and hit him with a pulse that finally got through his shield. His strength had faded, and his rage was burning itself out. The hit landed and he went flying. In an instant the Enchantress turned to Dori and shot a pulse out, aiming it for her heart. The pulse was strong enough to kill Dori.

But something had started happening to her that no one could quite explain. The glow from the emerald started to dance through her hand and up her arm. It didn't hurt or zap, as one would expect. Instead, it was comforting, like a friend wrapping her in a warm blanket. Up her arm it went and past her shoulder before it seemed to explode throughout her entire body. Dori was glowing as bright as the emerald, and the pulse that Enchantress had sent her way evaporated into nothing an inch from Dori's body.

Dori lifted her eyes to the witch and raised one eyebrow in defiance.

The Enchantress snapped, screaming out in anger, lifting her hand up as the dagger shot out of Rune's chest and landed back into her palm. Gunner immediately swore and pushed down as hard as he could on the wound, trying to slow down or stop the bleeding.

The Enchantress then let out one more war scream before lunging for Dori, intent on imbedding the dagger into her neck. But her final, fatal mistake was taking her eyes off Roran, who jumped right in front of her, grabbed her by the neck and lifted her up while squeezing.

"Time's up," he snarled.

"Roran!" Callan had stopped chanting and was standing a few feet away with the dagger Dori had used earlier to save Rune. He tossed it at Roran, who caught it and in one swift move jabbed it into the Enchantress's heart. She let out a deep below that reverberated off the walls, before Roran threw her to the ground. As she hit her body went limp.

Roran wasn't done with her yet. He stepped over to her, and with the last iota of magic that he had, he held his hand out and created the biggest, hottest fire ball he could manage. He then shot it at the Enchantress, who went up in magic flame and turned to cinders in mere seconds.

It was over. They had won. But it had come at a cost.

"Callan!" Gunner called out. Callan ran over and tried assessing how bad it was. Gunner's hands were soaked with Runes blood. Rune's face was getting paler with every passing moment. All the healers were either hiding in the forest or fleeing. Finding one would take far too long.

"We're gonna lose him," Gunner stated. Roran slowly walked up and fell to his knees beside them. He put a hand on Rune's arm.

"It's all my fault. I wasn't strong enough to fight the curse, and Rune paid the price." Roran was about to continue when a bright glow entered his peripheral vision. Squinting as he looked over at Dori, who's entire focus was on the man lying on the floor. The man that had given her the heart he didn't think he possessed.

Dori walked over to where they were at, still holding the emerald out in her hand. Thought wasn't present, everything was coming naturally to her, as if muscle memory knew what she had to do. In her trance like state Dori knelt beside Rune, tears falling down her face and dripping onto her shirt. With her empty hand she brushed his hair away from his eyes and cupped his face.

Knowing she didn't mean Rune any harm, Callan backed far enough away as to not be in her way. Gunner, who was on the other side of Rune, kept his hands on the wound, but stared at Dori, knowing something powerful was about to happen.

Roran, kneeling beside Gunner, watched carefully as the woman who fell from the sky stroked his brother's face. The emerald itself started to pulse and yet Dori wouldn't pull her hand away from Rune. Her fingertips brushed his dry and bloody lips. It wasn't that long ago that she was kissing him under the dancing lights in the sky. And now his soul was trying to leave this world.

The hand that held the crystal lowered, but the crystal stayed hovering in its spot. Dori used both of her hands to lightly grab Rune's face, lowering her own lips to his.

She kissed him once, to say goodbye. And then she kissed him one more time, but when she did a pulse went through her heart and the glowing green essence started flowing from her body into Rune's. The power of it entering his body jolted Gunner away.

Once every scrap of energy had left her body, Dori let go of him and collapsed to the side. The power started pulsing throughout Rune's body, in rhythm with a heartbeat. Ba bump. Ba bump. Ba bump.

His eyes shop open. His mouth shot open, and he took a deep breath before a stream of green power pulsed out of his mouth, into the ceiling, and into nothingness. The emerald floating beside Dori disintegrated piece by piece until it was nothing more than a pile of ash on the floor.

Rune started coughing and it knocked everyone into action. All four of them jumped back over to Rune. Gunner went to manage the blood flow from the wound, only to discover that it had disappeared. Whatever had been flowing through Rune had healed the wound. Roran grabbed for his wrist to check his pulse.

Callan slid over on his knees to check on Dori just as she was trying to sit up.

"Take it easy." Gunner stated as Rune tried sitting up. He didn't know everything that had happened, but it felt like a stone wall was dropped on his body. Things were still a bit fuzzy, but looking around at all the debris that surrounded them, he could tell he missed one hell of a battle.

Chapter 26

The next two days went by in a blur for Dori. After taking a few moments to assess any injuries caused by Briella and the Enchantress, it was determined that they all made it out of the battle mostly unharmed. The throne room, on the other hand, had been blown to pieces, chunks of stone littered the floor, as did the bodies of the Enchantress's army.

Slowly Roran, Rune, Callan, Gunner, and Dori exited the throne room and went searching for others. The rebellion had done a good job in the streets, making sure not to kill any guard that was under a spell, and to only disable them.

Before night came that first night there was a split. Some folks decided that, despite the Enchantress not being in power anymore, they would never fully feel like the city was a safe home. Those people made their way back into the forest for the night, promising to be back in the morning to help the clean-up of the city.

Others decided it was time to reclaim the city they called home. That group started clearing out residences and fixing them up enough to shelter them for the night. Anyone who didn't have a safe place to sleep was welcome in the castle, where blankets and pillows were provided from storage.

Roran and Rune were trying to come up with a way to get rid of the vines when Elowynn walked out of the forest and into the castle. Slowly she worked her magic, lifting her arms and chanting in a low voice. One by one the vines that had taken over the castle started to pull away and shrivel. Within the hour the castle was clear, leaving room in hallways and the front entrance for anyone who didn't have a bed. Dori went from person to person, making sure no one needed anything. Exhaustion hit her and she ended up passing out in one of the hallways.

When she woke, she was lying in a soft bed, on top of the blankets but covered up with a few spare jackets. Rune was lying beside her, his back to her, snoring away. The sight made her smile. After everything he went through, he was finally getting some rest.

No one had seen the elite munchkies since the Enchantress was defeated. Rumours floated around that they fled to the mountains once they realized they were on the losing side.

That second day was all about cleaning and clearing the city and the castle. In the light of day Roran was able to see how broken his city had become. He vowed not to fully rest until he made things right. It helped that, no matter what he did, at least one of his guardian brothers was by his side, helping.

Dori didn't have much time to talk to Roran one on one. They traded stories here and there about their experiences, but Roran was devoted to his people, and any time he spotted someone in need of something he would wander away from conversation. Dori didn't take offence; she knew the weight he felt in his heart would be there for awhile. He truly felt like he let his kingdom down and he would use every drop of energy he had to make things right. Looking out at his people and the way they reacted to him, Dori could see that they already forgave him, or maybe they never truly blamed him in the first place.

That second evening someone started up a bonfire just outside of the castle, where crowds gathered as the sun set. Looking around at the sea of people, a people who looked so obviously broken and tired, the one thing Dori saw in all of them was hope. Their eyes shined and their smiles gleamed. Dirt and dust may have covered them from their efforts at rebuilding, but the mood was light.

Right in the middle of the joyous festivities were Gunner and Callan, handing out refreshments provided by Roran to his people. They were surrounded by people trying to get their attention and, to their credit, they took the time to listen to every citizen. Some stories were of triumph, and some were of sorrow. But every person that had a story was made to feel important.

Dori felt a tap on her shoulder and, as she turned around, she found Rune standing there. Without saying a word, Rune offered her his hand. Dori reached out and took it, letting him pull her away from the crowd to a secluded bench. They could still see the firelight, but the voices were dulled. Dori sat down, looking at Rune, waiting to see if this was going to be a good conversation, or a bad one.

Chapter 27

R une grunted once or twice, trying to clear his throat. He had gone over this multiple times in his head, and still, he didn't know how to start talking to her. Dori smiled over at him, and, in typical Dori fashion, she reached over and took his hand in hers without hesitation. Rune looked down at their hands, and then up at her face. In that moment he knew exactly what he wanted to say to her.

"Dori, the woman who fell from the sky, the woman who saved this land and its people. The woman who showed me I still had a heart, and then stole it for herself. I could spend a thousand years thanking you for all that you have done, and still, it wouldn't be enough."

A lump started forming in Dori's throat as Rune started gently rubbing his thumb up and down the back of her hand.

"You have a choice to make, Dori. I won't make it for you. You can have Elowynn send you back to the life we stole you from. Your memories are your own, so if you want them to fade Elowynn can do that for you." The thought of going home and forgetting everything that had happened here, forgetting everyone she had met, didn't sit well with her and it caused a sour taste in her mouth.

"What's my other option?" Dori's voice came out quiet.

"The other option is you stay, here. It doesn't have to be with me, but you would stay. The life you left doesn't sound all that appealing, if you ask me, but I want you to make sure you have given it thought. There are people in your world that will notice you've gone. They will probably look for you, not that they would ever find you. You would be here, living out your life." Part of Rune didn't want to hand her the option, knowing that if she chose to leave back to her own world, it would rip his heart out more successfully than the Enchantress had. There would be no fixing it at that point. But as someone who had spent the last decade unable to live the life he wanted, Rune knew he would never take free will away from her. Dori would always have a choice.

"And if I stay, what does that mean for us?" Dori knew the time for dancing around the situation was over. For her to get real answers she would have to ask real questions.

"What do you want it to mean?" He questioned her.

Dori took a moment to pause so she could look inside herself. What did she really want from Rune, long term? Would he even be up for what she wanted? What if, after a few weeks, he wasn't as excited to be sharing his life with her? Just because she was the one to help save it all didn't mean she felt like she was owed his heart. Was it worth giving up her entire life for? Her brows creased as she internally went back and forth on what she truly wanted. Rune watched her for a moment, knowing where her hesitancy was coming from. He reached out and cupped her chin with his hand, lifting it up so that she was looking at him.

"Dori, listen carefully to me. I want to be very clear. I gave you my heart. That is yours now, unconditionally. Whether or not you stay with me, whether or not you stay in this land. My heart is yours. If you stay, and if you so desire, I would have you with me every day it still beats. I love you with every ounce of it. You brought it back to life, and I want to spend the rest of my nights under the stars showing you just how much you mean to me. What you must decide is if you are willing to give me your heart in return."

Looking into Rune's eyes Dori knew she would never spend another night underneath a different sky than him. The thought of being worlds apart forever was almost to much for her heart to bare. Dori hadn't expected him, she hadn't even wanted him when she first got here. But day by day, inch by inch, he wormed his way into her heart. To say that he was her soulmate wasn't enough. It wasn't just that their souls were meant to meet, they were meant to merge. Their souls were meant to collide to create something new, something magical. Even now, just sitting beside him, she could feel the vibrations of his aura calling to her. Rune's love swallowed her whole, like gravity it was a force she was unprepared to fight. Looking into his eyes in that moment, Dori knew the choice she was going to make.

"Rune, I'm not going anywhere. Not back home, not anywhere in this land. Nowhere that you aren't." A shaky breath left his mouth as he pulled her closer, using his thumb to brush the hair out of her face.

"Your soul spoke to mine and pulled me from the depths of hell. I touch you and it's like touching the sun. Warmth surrounds me, I feel light and love, and I know that everything will be okay." Rune had never been good at expressing his emotions, but for Dori he couldn't help but try. From the tears falling down Dori's face, it was clear it was working.

"I love you, Rune. Everything about you is lovable, especially your heart." She whispered to him as she put her hand on his chest above where his heart was.

Rune couldn't hold back anymore as he pulled her in for a kiss. It wasn't a light kiss, or a peck on the lips. Rune pulled her in with a ferocity that excited her. Passion sparked between the two of them as their tongues danced together. Dori would never get enough of him, of how he felt against her, of how he tasted. After a moment Rune pulled away, he had one more thing to talk to her about and it was important enough that it couldn't wait any longer.

"The people of the forest asked me if I would lead them. Despite the sisters being gone, they don't feel comfortable going back to the way things were. They've all created their own village in the trees. Roran assured them that he wouldn't make them vacate the home they made for themselves. But they need a leader in their community, and they asked me if I wanted to be it." Rune explained. It didn't surprise Dori in the slightest. Rune was made to be a leader, smart and compassionate.

"You would make a good leader to those people. You would keep them safe." Dori went to start kissing him again, but Rune, unable to stop smiling, held her back as he still had one thing to get out.

"They asked about you, too." He stated.

That caused her to stop, pulling back to look him in the eyes. "Me?"

"Yes. I don't think you understand the absolute change you've made in people's lives. They see you as a kind soul. Someone to lend a helping hand. You talk truth, but never in a way to hurt. You are full of compassion, something they haven't had enough of this past decade. The question is, would you? Would you lead them with me? Move to one of those treetop huts and set up house with me?" The last few words came out quieter as Rune tried to prepare himself for any outcome. He didn't want to assume she would be up for the challenge. Dori sat back for a moment, taking a much-needed breath.

"This is a lot …" Help lead people, a community in a land that she didn't know existed a few weeks ago?

"It is." That's all he said. He didn't try to sway her one way or the other. He didn't beg her to stay, he didn't try and guilt her into it. He sat there, by her side, allowing her to make the choice of her own volition. It felt like his heart was jumping out of his chest. Waiting for her to reject or accept the offer had him holding his breath. If she rejected it, he would still find a way to lead the people, but he wouldn't tie her to the forest.

Glancing at the forest in the distance, watching the leaves sway lightly in the wind, hearing the laughter and happiness around the campfire, Dori had nothing to offer to Rune but a smile.

"On one condition … the hut we move into has to have a clear view of the night sky, so that the dancing lights can be seen from our bed." Dori grinned at him.

Rune almost fell of the bench. In a way, he didn't want to allow himself to hope, and yet here she was, ready to embrace all of it.

"What?" He needed her to say it one more time. He had to be sure.

"You have straw in your ears? I'm saying yes. To you. To them. To all of it. Yes, to moving to the forest, to helping lead the people. Yes, to being by your side day in, and day out. Yes, to making love under the stars."

Rune didn't let her finish, instead grabbing her face and covering it with small kisses that had her giggling. Dori used her hands to pull him closer, bringing her lips to his. That was when his heart, his once broken and cursed heart, was finally healed and beating strong.

Celebrations happened all throughout the land in the week after the defeat of the Enchantress. But none of it compared to the celebrating happening at the castle.

The vines had been cleared away, the spelled guards had all been cured, the dust and dirt and broken walls had all been cleared up and patched up. Most of the injuries had healed and it was time to bring some happiness to the people.

They were calling it a coronation. King Roran had finally fully returned, and his people wanted to celebrate with him.

The night of the event, after the official re-crowning, King Roran, sitting on his throne, was looking out at the room filled with his people. The people that made it through the worst of it and came out on the other side. Despite the dark things they had all seen and been through, they were all there to celebrate.

Standing in front of him were the four biggest reasons the Enchantress was able to be defeated.

"I want to thank all of you for coming here tonight. I want to thank you for always being loyal, even when it was hard.

I appreciate each and every one of you for the sacrifices you had to endure to make it through. But there are a few of you that I would like to thank personally. First, Guardian Callan. I would like to thank you for your loyalty, and for your quick wit in dire situations. Your knowledge of the magics of this land, and your confidence in knowing when you needed to ask for help was unparalleled. To you I would like to extend the offer of being named hand of the King. I want you in the room when tough decisions are being made, I want your perspective and opinions on the little things, but also on the big things, like rebuilding this kingdom. Do you accept?"

Callan was slightly surprised at the offer. It was a position of honor and trust. Gunner nudged him slightly.

"Oh yes, yes, I accept. Thank you for the honor, King Roran." Callan bowed before Roran, as Roran pinned his sigil to Callan's right breast pocket. Callan stood up and shook the hand Roran offered. Callan immediately turned while the crowd cheered, accepting a hug from Gunner. Before much else could happen, Roran held his arms up and everyone quieted.

"Next, Guardian Gunner. I want to thank you for your endless bravery in taking back the castle, and in being instrumental in sending out the signal for help. Defying the Enchantress straight to her face was bold. To you I would like to offer the position of lead General. I want you leading my armies into, and out of, any battles that may come our way. We had gotten lazy before the Enchantress slipped in here. I don't want it happening again. You will lead my men and show them the courage it takes to keep this kingdom and our people safe. Will you accept?"

It was Gunner's turn to look stunned. Roran was treating him like he hadn't spent the last decade hiding under a table at every loud noise. But still, looking into Roran's eyes, Gunner could see the sincerity and trust Roran had in him. Straightening his spine, Gunner responded.

"I won't let you down, King Roran." Gunner knelt down as Roran pinned a battle emblem on his right breast pocket. Gunner stood slowly, and before thinking about it, launched a hug at Roran, who merely laughed in joy and returned the hug. The crowd cheered once more and anyone that could reach him was patting Gunner on the back, Callan included. Once again, after letting Gunner have his moment, King Roran raised his hands for quiet.

"Guardian Rune. I had a special title for you as well, but from the whispers I hear, you may have already accepted a new title. Leader of the forest people, is that correct?"

Rune looked apprehensive, it wasn't his intention to insult Roran, but he truly thought it was for the best.

"Yes, sir. Sorry, I should have talked to you about it ..." Roran waved his hand in dismissal at the apology.

"Nonsense, it's a move that makes sense. Rune, the people that still live in that forest, they won't trust easily. Living in the town, anywhere near the castle, it's to much for them. I don't hold their trauma against them. They need time to heal on their own, away from everything that went wrong. You represent hope to them, and they trust you. Why wouldn't I want that throughout the lands? Now, I do have one title for you, if you'll accept it. Emissary to the Forest Folk. I won't bother you much, but once in awhile I'll ask you to come to the castle for diplomatic discussions. There is more than enough room and resources in this land for all, but it will only work if we keep communications open between us. Do you accept?"

Dori held her breath and Rune took a quick second to look over at her. She gave him a half smile of encouragement.

"Yes, King Roran. I accept."

Roran stuck his hand out and Rune grabbed it, using it to pull Roran into a tight hug.

"Thank you, my friend. You saved us all," Roran whispered in Rune's ear, and it took everything in Rune to keep his emotions at bay. Tears still flooded his eyes. Roran stepped back, clapping him in the shoulder.

"You would think I was done, as my three Guardians all have new titles and positions. However, there is one more person here that deserves something. Dori, please step forward."

Dori's faced paled as Callan and Gunner pushed her forward, until she was directly in front of Roran. Her hands were shaking, unsure of what Roran was going to say to her.

"Guardian Dori."

Dori's head snapped up as she looked on in confusion.

"Yes, you heard me right. Guardian Dori. This is the first time in our history that a guardian emerged that was not from this land. But that's exactly what you are. You came here, a stranger to this land, and with every breathe in your body you defended it, and its people, without asking for anything in return. If I'm not mistaken you've already gotten the greatest gift anyone could ask for."

Roran turned to Rune for a moment before looking back.

"I also know that any offer to send you back to the land you came from would be met with polite refusal. I do want to offer you this, though. This land, this kingdom, is now your home. You are not the outsider, not anymore. The forest folk have accepted you as one of their leaders, which I very much support. All I have left to offer you is this, friendship. And my eternal gratitude. For you Dori, for saving my people." Roran took a small step back and then bowed, lowering himself down on one knee. Within moments every person in the room followed along suit, until Dori was the only one standing, tears streaming down her face.

"I don't deserve this. I only did what was right," Dori whispered. Roran stood, smiling at her, taking her hand in his.

"That is the hardest thing to do at times. And you still did it spectacularly!" Roran grabbed her in hug, followed by Callan, Gunner, and of course Rune. The room exploded in cheers as

Dori looked around, thinking to herself, there's no place like home.

Gratitude

I want to start off by thanking everyone who has supported me this year on my new journey as a published author. It means the world to me that you, the readers, are becoming invested in my characters and my stories. It's truly a dream come true.

I want to thank Frank L. Baum for creating this world that I loved and cherished as a child. I am excited to be dipping a toe in and carving out my own little pocket of Oz.

I want to thank my family for putting up with the late writing nights and weekends where I was stuck in the basement, formatting and editing. Without their support this book simply would not exist.

Lastly, I want to thank all of my proofreaders, ARC readers, and my editor, Katie. You all help my writing to strengthen and you help the confidence within myself grow.

About the Author

Chelsea was born in the Hundred Acre Woods. As a child she became a world traveler without every having to leave her house. Narnia, Oz, Wonderland, and Neverland were a few of her favorite places to be. In her spare time she would tame dragons, battle trolls and ogres, fight pirates, and find magic in the most unexpected places. Now that she's an adult she is overjoyed at being able to bring her children along on these adventures.

Where can you find Chelsea?

Where can you find Chelsea? Other than with her head in the clouds, here is where she spends her time:

Tiktok – @author.chelsea.b
Instagram – @author.chelsea.b
Threads -@author.chelsea.b
www.authorchelseabiddiscombe.ca

Translations

- Abdita tempore, latens in spatio. Auxilium vocamus – Lost in time, hidden in space. We call for help. (Prologue)

- Emohek ilecal pon sereht – There's no place like home (Chapter 25)

Other Works by Chelsea Biddiscombe

Awakening Fate (Book 1 in the Intertwined Trilogy) – An urban fantasy twist on the classic Little Red Riding Hood tale. Currently available in e-book and paperback formats. For more information, visit www.authorchelseabiddiscombe.ca

Made in United States
North Haven, CT
25 November 2024

60850286R00145